"Are you sure you're all right, Grace?"

Kaleb was the kind of guy who would listen attentively and do his best to comfort her. And the comforting was what worried Grace. It would be so easy to fall into his strong arms and believe that all was right with the world.

So, for her boss's sake as much as her own, she'd just have to fake it. "Yeah. I'm just a little tired, that's all."

"I hope you're not getting sick." He moved toward her, his concern mounting.

"I'm fine. I just…" *Tell him. Give the guy a chance.* "I didn't sleep well last night." No fibbing there.

Wiping his hands on a shop rag, he continued to study her. "That would explain the bags under your eyes."

Did he just…? "Bags? What do you mean?"

He laughed. "There's the spitfire we all know and love."

Love?

Still laughing, he closed the distance and gave her a hug. "Sleep well, Grace." He smelled of fresh air and masculinity. She missed him as soon as he stepped away. "And remember, I'm always here if you need me."

It took **Mindy Obenhaus** forty years to figure out what she wanted to do when she grew up. But once God called her to write, she never looked back. She's passionate about touching readers with biblical truths in an entertaining, and sometimes adventurous, manner. Mindy lives in Texas with her husband and kids. When she's not writing, she enjoys cooking and spending time with her grandchildren. Find more at mindyobenhaus.com.

Books by Mindy Obenhaus

Love Inspired

The Doctor's Family Reunion
Rescuing the Texan's Heart
A Father's Second Chance
Falling for the Hometown Hero

Falling for the Hometown Hero

Mindy Obenhaus

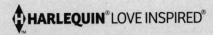
HARLEQUIN® LOVE INSPIRED®

Recycling programs
for this product may
not exist in your area.

LOVE INSPIRED BOOKS

ISBN-13: 978-0-373-71961-7

Falling for the Hometown Hero

www.Harlequin.com

Printed in U.S.A.

He heals the brokenhearted
and binds up their wounds.
—*Psalms* 147:3

To all of our wounded warriors.
May God bless you richly.

Acknowledgments

For Your glory, Lord.

To my amazing husband, Richard. I am so blessed to have you in my life. Your support carries me through the toughest of times. Thank you for countless brainstorming lunches and for your desire to help me achieve my goals.

To my guys, Ryan and Michael: y'all endured countless leftovers, pizza and pot pies and had to forego many a homemade treat for this one. Thanks for allowing me to do what I do.

Thanks to Lisa Jordan for stepping in the gap and allowing me the privilege of being your "Rachel."

To Becky Yauger: missed you, girl. So glad you're back.

Thank you Robert and Mary Ellen Bolton, motorcycle couple extraordinaire, for enlightening me on the world of motorcycle travel.

Many thanks to Vanessa Villanueva, LVN, and Yvonne Brefo, RN, for the medical info.

To Brandy Ross for rockin' the pink shirt and putting up with the silliest of questions.

To Ted and Betty Wolfe for your friendship and guidance.

To Noah Galloway: I knew nothing about you when I started this book, but seeing you on *Dancing with the Stars* gave me so much more insight. You are an inspiration to all of us.

Chapter One

His dream had come true.

As a kid growing up in Ouray, Colorado, Kaleb Palmer dreamed of owning a Jeep tour company. Of sharing the history and beauty of the San Juan Mountains with others. That dream had kept him going during the darkest time of his life and, finally, it had become a reality.

The online reviews said Mountain View Tours had terrible service.

The whispered words of a passerby echoed through his mind as he leaned the freshly painted wooden sign that read Under New Ownership beside the entrance. If they only knew. He'd had plenty of experience overcoming adversity.

Returning to the open bay of the garage, Kaleb tugged a shop rag from the back pocket of his jeans and rubbed the smudges of red paint from his fingers.

Excitement coursed through his veins, as it had so many times since purchasing Mountain View Tours a few months ago. It would take time to rebuild the company's tarnished reputation. And with the Jeeping season lasting less than five months, time wasn't exactly on Kaleb's side. There were loans to be paid, and he would not let his investors down. How could he when they'd given him the courage and financial backing to follow his dream?

The late afternoon sun had him rolling up the sleeves of his tan work shirt as he looked out over Main Street, surveying Ouray's colorful Victorian buildings. Now that May had arrived, businesses that had closed for the winter were primping for the upcoming high season. All over town, folks were painting, planting flowers and sprucing up in preparation for the thousands of people who would flock to the Switzerland of America over the next few months.

Out of the corner of his eye, he noticed a black motorcycle easing alongside the curb in front of his business. A potential customer, perhaps. Either way, his pulse kicked up a notch. This wasn't just any motorcycle. It was a sleek BMW K 100 LT, a touring motorcycle that put all other motorcycles to shame in his book.

As a teenager, he yearned for the day he'd own one and had even contemplated purchasing that very model once he left the army. How he'd longed to conquer the Million Dollar Highway that wound its way through the mountains south of town, leaning the machine into every hairpin curve.

Of course, that was back when he had two legs.

Absently rubbing his left thigh, where his stump and prosthetic met, he watched the leather-clad, undeniably female figure dismount the bike that was bigger than her. Was she traveling alone or waiting for someone to join her?

The woman removed her helmet then, allowing her dark hair to tumble halfway down her back.

Kaleb's breath left him. He swallowed hard, the reaction taking him by surprise. He couldn't remember the last time a woman had that kind of effect on him. Especially one he'd never met.

She looked up and down the street, allowing him a

glimpse of her face. Much younger than he would have expected. And while he couldn't put his finger on it, there was something about her that intrigued him. The determined square of her shoulders, the confidence in her stance.

Again wiping his hands, he pretended not to notice as she left her helmet on the bike and started in the direction of Mountain View Tours' front office. Maybe this was the day he'd book his first tour.

Leaving his fanciful thoughts in the shop along with his rag, he slid past one of his new tour trucks—bright blue and specially outfitted with open-air seating for nine—opened the office door and went inside.

"Afternoon." He moved behind the crude particleboard reception counter. "Welcome to Mountain View Tours."

"Hi." The woman unzipped her black leather jacket, her smile wide as she took in the front office. "I'm looking for Kaleb Palmer."

A dozen scenarios sprang to his mind as to why a beautiful motorcycle-driving woman would be looking for him. A relative of one of the men who'd been with him that fateful day in the Afghan desert, perhaps?

"I'm Kaleb. What can I do for you?"

She opened her mouth, then closed it without saying a word, her expression seemingly perplexed. Her hazel eyes fell to the concrete floor, before bouncing back to his. "Sorry. I guess I expected someone older." Pink tinged her cheeks as she held out her hand. "I'm Grace McAllen."

Her firm grip wasn't the only thing that surprised him. Granted, he'd shared only one phone call and a couple of emails with Grace, but with her husky voice, military background and no-nonsense approach to business, he never imagined his new office manager would be so...pretty.

Scratching his head, he glanced at the calendar on the

wall. "I must be mixed up on my days. I wasn't expecting you until tomorrow."

"No. You're correct." She took a step back. "I just pulled into town and thought I'd drop by before checking in at the campground."

"You're staying at the campground?" Not something he would have expected from a single woman.

"Why not? I have a camper."

He peered out the window, noting the low-profile trailer hitched to the back of her motorcycle.

"Don't let appearances fool you." She'd obviously caught his stare. "It's a pop-up. Much bigger than it looks."

That was good, because it still looked pretty small to him. However, he was six-three and liked his space.

"Cool." He turned his attention back to Grace. "So would you like to start working tomorrow, then? Or would you prefer a day to familiarize yourself with the town?"

"Tomorrow is fine."

"Good." He rounded the counter to join her in the open space that was flanked by a vintage Coke machine and a particleboard brochure rack that matched the desk. "The faster we can get you up to speed, the better I'll feel. And I figure the best way to start is with a couple of informal tours. I'll give you a firsthand look at what we do and, in turn, better equip you to assist customers."

"Sounds reasonable." She shoved her hands into the back pockets of her jeans and looked him in the eye. "I haven't been to Ouray before, but if the drive up here is any indication, I can hardly wait."

"I like your enthusiasm." Kaleb had prayed long and hard that God would lead him to the right employees. Those who would share his love for this area and pass that zeal on to customers. "Most of the passes are still closed, but we can make a run up to Yankee Boy Basin. Which also happens to be one of the area's most popular destinations."

"What time should I be here?"

"Eight o'clock too early?"

"Not at all."

Nodding, he leaned an elbow against the counter and tried not to stare at his newest employee. The way her silky brown hair spilled over her shoulders and the hint of a dimple in her right cheek.

He cleared his throat. "The front office here is where you'll spend most of your time. That's my office there." He motioned to the small room at his left.

Her brow puckered as she scrutinized the area. "It has promise. A few simple cosmetic changes could brighten this space considerably."

"Cosmetic changes?" What was she talking about? "The place is perfectly fine. A bit rustic, but in some circles, the rustic look is all the rage. I put my money where it really mattered. Upgrading the rental Jeeps and tour trucks."

His former boss, Mountain View Tours' previous owner, had been a notorious cheapskate, barely putting any money into his vehicles and, in turn, ruining the company's once-glowing reputation. A reputation Kaleb was determined to restore.

Grace smiled politely. "Okay, then——"

"I got a lollipop!" The announcement came from Kaleb's four-year-old nephew, Jack, as he barreled through the front door in cowboy boots and shorts, lips bright red from the candy he proudly held in his hand.

"Is that for me?" He scooped the child into his arms before sticky fingers could make contact with anything or anyone.

"No." Jack squirmed and giggled, his brown eyes alight with amusement. "You hafta get a haircut to get one."

"Jackson Kaleb, you are supposed to wait for Mommy." Sami, Kaleb's sister, looked fit to be tied as she strode into the office, fists clenched at her sides, her blond ponytail escaping its confines. "What if there had been a car coming?"

Kaleb glared at his nephew. "Jack…? Did you run across the street by yourself?"

"But I wanted to show you." The sincerity of Jack's words settled into Kaleb's heart.

After falling prey to an IED in Afghanistan, Kaleb had returned to Ouray just before Jack was born. He soon discovered that holding Jack and spending time with him was the best medicine Kaleb could have asked for, taking his focus off of his inabilities and forging a special bond. A bond Kaleb hoped to one day share with a child of his own.

He softened his expression. "Safety first, soldier. You know that." He regarded his new employee. "Jack, this is Grace. She's going to be working here this summer, so you'll probably see a lot of her."

"Hi, Gwace." Jack popped his lollipop into his mouth.

"How's it going, Jack?" Smiling, she waved and Kaleb saw a spark in her eyes that had him suspecting she liked kids. Yet as quick as it came to life, it was gone.

Suddenly shy, Jack laid his head against Kaleb's shoulder.

"Hi, Grace." His sister extended her hand. "I'm Sami, Kaleb's sister, part-time helper around here and mom to this little mischief maker." She poked a thumb toward Jack.

"Nice to meet you."

"Grace just got into town." Kaleb smoothed a hand across his nephew's back, the sweet smell of strawberry enveloping them both.

"Welcome to Ouray." Sami gave Grace her full attention. "This your first time to visit us?"

"Yes." Grace's eyes drifted to the window. "And it's even prettier than I imagined."

"That it is." Sami let go a contented sigh, before addressing Grace again. "Where are you from?"

"All over." Grace faced his sister. "I grew up a military brat then joined the navy right out of high school."

"Wow!" Sami's dark brown eyes flashed with excitement. For all of her contentment, Kaleb knew his sister longed to travel. "I bet you've been to some exotic places."

"I suppose. But few as beautiful as what I saw driving in today." Grace hesitated, a puzzled expression on her face. "I'm sorry—have I said that already?" She looked from Sami to Kaleb. "It really is true, though." The conviction in Grace's voice was hard to miss. And precisely what Kaleb needed to set Mountain View Tours on the road to becoming a thriving business once again.

Anticipation flooded through him as he set Jack on the floor. "Grace, you haven't even seen the tip of the iceberg. Just wait till you find out what's in store for you."

Grace, you are such a goober.

Gravel crunched beneath her tires as she backed her bike into the tree-canopied campsite that butted against the jagged sandstone surface of the mountainside.

When she'd talked with Kaleb Palmer on the telephone, his deep voice had her envisioning him to be somewhere upwards of fifty years old, with a moderate paunch around his midsection, wearing an old trucker hat and coveralls. Instead, he was only a few years older than her twenty-eight years, well built, with biceps bigger than her thighs. Not to mention those gray-green eyes that had her gushing like a schoolgirl.

She cringed, recalling how many times she'd used the

word *beautiful* or some variation thereof. Even if she had
meant it, she probably came across as phony.

Much like her ex-husband. *It's all right, Grace. We've
got each other, and that's all we need.* Over the two years
that Grace had tried unsuccessfully to conceive, Aaron
had uttered those words month after stinking month. She'd
even started to believe him. Until he left her for his pregnant girlfriend.

Annoyed that she'd allowed her mind to wander down
that depressing path, she killed the engine, dropped the
kickstand and got off her motorcycle. After removing her
helmet, she surveyed the place that would be her home for
the next few months.

The showers weren't too far away, so that was a bonus.
Across the way, a large motor home was parked at an angle.
Several sites down from her, there was a silver Airstream
trailer and a few more RVs dotted the campground. Aside
from that, the place was empty. Something she was certain would change as they moved into summer.

Focusing on her own campsite, she noted the picnic
table and a small fire pit that doubled as a grill. A water
spigot and electrical box. Lifting her gaze, she studied the
mountains, many still topped with snow. Definitely something she wasn't used to seeing from the deck of an aircraft carrier. Or from the screened-in porch at her home
in Jacksonville, Florida.

She shook away the unwanted memories, dropped her
helmet and jacket atop the picnic table then tugged the
phone from her back pocket and sent a text to her sister,
letting her know she'd arrived safely. Thirty seconds later,
the phone rang and Lucy's name appeared on the screen.

Grace should have known her little sister wouldn't be
satisfied with a text.

"Hey, Luce."

"I told you to call me when you got there. Not text."

"Just trying to save time." Grace sat down at the table. "I haven't even set up camp yet."

"In that case, I'll cut you some slack. So… What do you think of Ouray?" Excitement laced Lucy's tone.

Her sister and mother had spent the summer after Dad's death up here and Lucy had fallen in love with the town. If only things had been that simple with their mother.

"In a word? Gorgeous. The pictures you showed me didn't even begin to do it justice."

"See? Didn't I tell you?"

"You did." Something she was certain Lucy would never let her forget.

"I think the change of scenery will do wonders for you, Grace. At the end of the summer, you'll feel like a new woman, refreshed and ready to conquer the world."

Conquering the world was exactly what Grace planned to do. Unfortunately, the ship the cruise line had assigned her to was in dry dock, undergoing renovations, and she wouldn't be setting sail as an excursions manager until late September. So, at Lucy's relentless urging, Grace reluctantly accepted a summer job in Ouray.

Using her finger, she traced the heart someone had carved into the wooden tabletop. "I hope so." After her divorce last year, she finished out her enlistment then discharged from the navy, eager to flee Jacksonville and start a new life. A life lived on her terms, not those of a God who'd turned His back on her.

"Have you been to see Mama yet?"

Grace's whole being sagged. That was the one aspect of this summer she was divided on. She knew she needed to reconnect with her mother, at least on some level, before heading out to sea. But seeing her mother meant she would also have to see *him*.

"No. Like I said, I have to set up camp."

"I still don't understand why you won't stay with Mama and Roger."

"You know why."

"Come on, Grace. They've been married for three years. Don't you think it's time you gave Roger a chance?"

"Not particularly." That would be like turning her back on her father.

"He's a good guy, Grace. He makes Mama happy."

"Perhaps." But how her mother could move on only a year after Daddy's death was something Grace would never understand. "Hey, look, I need to get things going here, so I'll talk to you later, Luce."

Grace ended the call, eager to be done with any and all talk of Roger, grabbed work gloves from her saddlebag and unhitched her trailer from her bike. With a firm grip on the tongue of the trailer, she maneuvered it back and to the right, a position that would afford her a nice view, as well as some privacy.

Forty-five minutes later, both her trailer and a separate canopy she'd use as a lounge/kitchen area were ready to go. Sure it was small, but compared to her cramped quarters on the aircraft carrier, it was the Taj Mahal.

She giggled then, remembering that was exactly what her father used to call it. When he was alive, he would take a monthlong road trip on his motorcycle every summer. Sometimes he'd go to bike rallies or visit her if she wasn't at sea. Wherever he went, though, this camper was his home away from home.

A tear spilled onto her cheek and she quickly wiped it away. If only he could be here now. Maybe then she wouldn't feel so alone. So vacant. He'd wrap her in one of his famous bear hugs and help her make sense of her life.

I miss you, Daddy.

She ducked under the canopy and collapsed in her favorite lawn chair, suddenly exhausted. The sun had barely risen when she pulled away from her sister's house in Flagstaff this morning. Lifting the lid on the cooler beside her, she snagged a Diet Dr Pepper and was just about to kick off her riding boots when she noticed the back tire on her motorcycle was flat.

"Are you kidding me?" She groaned, setting the unopened can on the cooler, and went to investigate. Once she removed the saddlebags, it didn't take her long to find the nail lodged into the tread. Thankfully, it would be an easy repair.

After pulling her hair into a quick ponytail, she opened the first saddlebag and dug through it, searching for a plug kit. Coming up empty-handed, she moved on to the next one. "Where are you?" She always carried at least two plug kits.

"Aha!" She pulled out the orange box and opened its lid.

Her heart dropped. Everything was there. The tools, the rubber cement… But no plugs.

She looked at her watch. Five thirty. What time did stores close around here anyway? She'd spotted a hardware store on her way in. Hopefully, they'd not only be open, but have what she needed, as well.

She tucked her saddlebags inside the tent, then briskly walked the six blocks to the hardware store.

"I'm sorry, but we're temporarily out of both the plugs and plug kits." The clerk's apologetic smile did little to comfort her. "But you could check with one of the Jeep tour places. They might be able to help you."

Seriously? A Jeep place?

Okay, so they had a lot of tires to worry about, but she was only familiar with one Jeep place and the idea of going back there again today didn't settle well. What if Kaleb thought she was one of those women who was merely look-ing for an excuse to return?

You could check with your mother.

Definitely not. Besides, she was planning to walk to work tomorrow.

What if there's an emergency, and you need your bike?

She blew out a frustrated breath. Logic left so much to be desired.

Trekking across the street, she swallowed her pride and walked into the somewhat dingy office of Mountain View Tours. A gallon or two of paint would do wonders for this place.

Kaleb stood behind the desk, his back to her. "Be right with you." The overhead fluorescent bulbs highlighted a bit of blond in his short sandy-brown hair.

She waited in silence, her anxiety building.

"Grace?" His smile was easy and he appeared almost happy to see her. "What are you doing here?"

"I have a flat on my bike. By any chance do you sell tire plugs?"

"No, we do not."

In that instant, her tire wasn't the only thing that was deflated. Oh, well. At least she was within walking dis-tance of work. She'd just have to wait for the hardware store to replenish their stock. Or check with one of those other Jeep places the clerk had mentioned.

"But I'd be happy to give you one."

Her gaze jerked to Kaleb's. "Really?"

"Mountain View Tours always takes care of their cus-tomers."

"I'm not a—"

"And their employees."

"Oh." Her cheeks grew warm and she turned her head to hide the reaction.

"I'll be right back." He rounded the counter and disappeared through the door that led to the garage. A minute later, he reappeared. "Here you go." He handed her a bag with three plugs. "You need any tools?"

"Those I have, so no—" she dared to look at him "—thank you."

"My pleasure." He glanced at the generic round wall clock behind the desk. "I'm about to lock up. I could give you a lift and help with that tire, if you like."

"Oh, that won't be—"

"Grace, a gentleman does not let an unaccompanied female fix her own flat tire."

"But—"

"No matter how capable she might be."

Again she felt herself blush. Totally weird since she couldn't remember the last time she'd blushed. Still, she didn't need or want Kaleb's help. She didn't like to rely on other people. She could take care of herself.

"Look, this wouldn't be the first plug I've done." No, it would be the second. "I can have it fixed—"

"Grace." The look he gave her left no room for question. Much like her commanding officer. "I'm coming to help you, and that's all there is to it."

Great. So her boss thought her a damsel in distress.

She'd just have to prove him wrong.

Chapter Two

Kaleb held the passenger door of his Jeep open as Grace, now sporting a ponytail and a plain gray T-shirt, reluctantly climbed inside. Clearly, she was a strong, independent woman, evidenced by the fact that she drove a motorcycle and was staying alone at the campground. Still, he preferred to make sure things were done and done right.

"This really isn't necessary, you know." Grace's tone held a hint of annoyance, which he chose to ignore.

"So you've said." He tossed the door closed, continued around to the driver's side and hopped in. "But given that you're new in town, it's only logical that I should offer my newest employee a hand. People helping people. That's how we are in Ouray."

While she stared out the window, he started the vehicle, crossed Main Street and headed down Seventh Avenue.

Grace jerked her head in his direction. "How do you know which way to go?"

"Easy." He eyed the cross streets for traffic. "There are only two RV parks within walking distance of Main Street. I saw you coming up Seventh before turning into the hardware store." He shrugged. "Simple process of elimination."

She didn't say anything, but her narrowed eyes told him

she wasn't necessarily pleased with his observation. Not that he cared. War had taught him to pay attention to detail.

He made a right onto Oak Street, gravel crunching beneath the Jeep's heavy-duty tires. "I'll have to rely on you to direct me to your campsite, though. Either that or drive around until I see your motorcycle."

"Wouldn't take you long. I'm just a few sites into the campground."

Sure enough. Once they'd passed the office on the right and showers to their left, he spotted her motorcycle and camper.

Grace was halfway out the door before he even brought the Jeep to a stop in front of her campsite. She moved around the vehicle and continued straight on to her tent.

Women. He hoped she wasn't going to be this stubborn about everything.

She had a tire that needed fixing, though, and he intended to do just that.

He stepped out of the Jeep and retrieved his toolbox from the backseat. When he turned around, Grace reappeared—carrying a toolbox.

Uh-oh. *Tread lightly, Palmer.*

"For the record—" he set his toolbox on the ground beside her motorcycle "—I'm not a chauvinist or anything. I just like to make sure things are done correctly."

She set her toolbox down with a thud, then crossed her arms over her chest. "You don't think I can do it correctly?"

"I didn't say that." He eyeballed the flat tire, spotting the nail right away. "It'll just make me feel better, that's all."

Kneeling on his good knee, he lifted the lid on his toolbox and reached for a pair of pliers. "Do you have a compressor or something to inflate the tire once it's repaired?"

She continued to glare at him. "Wouldn't take a road trip without one."

"Glad to hear it." Using the pliers, he pulled the nail from the tire. "You said you had a plug tool?"

Her brow shot up. "You mean you don't have one?"

He pondered the spitfire staring down at him. "Actually…" He dug through his toolbox until he found his own plug kit tucked in the bottom. "Yep." He held it up.

Threading the thick rubbery plug through the eye of the tool that was best described as a giant needle with a handle, he glanced over his shoulder.

"That's an interesting setup you've got there." Definitely not like the campers he was used to seeing. Instead of the pop-up going up and out on both ends, it went up and then out on one side, making it look like a tent sitting on a wagon.

"Thanks." Arms still crossed, she watched as he jammed the tool into the tire. "It belonged to my dad."

Melancholy wove its way through her last statement, telling him far more than her words.

"I take it he's no longer with us?"

"Cancer." She scraped a booted foot across the gravel. "Four years ago."

Even with the distance of time, her grief was evident.

"He must have been a young man." Kaleb pulled the tool back out then grabbed a pair of cutters to trim the excess plug.

"Fifty-six."

That had to be difficult. Losing someone who, by all counts, was in the prime of their life. He knew what that was like. Tossing his tools back into the box, he stood and looked at her, his annoyance fading. "I'm sorry."

"Don't be. It wasn't your fault." Despite a momentary chink, her armor was back in place. "I'll get that compressor."

She turned and again headed for her tent, but not before he noticed the sadness in her hazel eyes. Beyond the striking mix of green, brown and gold, there lurked something that intrigued him all the more.

For all of Grace's toughness, it seemed her heart was as tender as the wildflowers that blanketed the mountains in late July. Those that endured the harshest of winters only to flourish and grow more beautiful.

Not at all like Gina, his ex-fiancée. She'd wilted as soon as the storm clouds rolled in.

The hum of an electric engine drew his attention. Looking up the road, he spotted Luann Carter zooming toward him in her signature red golf cart, her grin as wide as ever.

She slowed to stop in front of him. "I thought that was you, Kaleb." She hopped out, scurried around the cart and greeted him with a hug. "It's always a joy to see you."

"How's it going?" He released the sixty-some-year-old redhead and peered down at her. Luann was a short one all right. Not even reaching five feet tall. But what she lacked in height, she more than made up for in spirit.

"Just wonderful. And how 'bout yourself? I'm sure you're so busy you're havin' to turn away customers."

"I wish things were that good, Luann. But I'm hoping they'll pick up after Memorial Day."

"That reminds me. " She wagged a finger his way. "Make sure you bring me some brochures. I want to have plenty on hand so I can tell everyone about the *new* Mountain View Tours."

He couldn't help smiling. Seemed the whole town had rallied around him, willing him to bring this fledgling company back from the brink of disaster. He was determined to show that their faith in him wasn't unfounded.

"I'll be sure and do that just as soon as I get them printed." Of course, before he could do that, he had to have someone design them. Add that to the long list of things he had yet to do.

"Well, hello there." Luann's attention shifted to somewhere behind him.

He turned to find Grace, compressor in hand. "Luann, I'd like you to meet my new office manager. Grace McAllen, this is Luann Carter. She and her husband, Bud, own the campground."

"Pleasure to meet you." Grace smiled at the older woman. "I think I met your husband when I checked in."

Luann waved a hand. "Probably. I've been out running errands most of the afternoon." Her assessing gaze skimmed over Grace. "So you'll be working with Kaleb?"

"Yes, ma'am."

"Well, let me tell you, sugar, this is probably one of the finest young men you could ever work for." Luann rested a hand on his arm. "He is kind, generous, respectful..." She hesitated a moment, then forged on. "Ol' Bud and I were having some car trouble back this winter and, well, things were a little tight financially." She gently squeezed his arm. "So Kaleb here fixed it for us and didn't charge us a thing, 'cept for the parts."

Warmth crept up Kaleb's neck as Grace's focus shifted to him.

"Poor fella spent two days in that freezing-cold garage and never asked for anything more than one of my coconut cream pies."

He cleared his throat. "Grace, if you ever have one of Luann's coconut pies, you'll understand that it was a very fair trade."

Luann playfully swatted him, her own cheeks turning pink. "Oh, stop, you."

Grace watched the two of them, a smile lifting the corners of her mouth. "You have a lovely campground, Luann."

"Thank you, sugar." Luann's phone whistled. She tugged it from the clip attached to the pocket of her cargo pants and looked at the screen. "Looks like Bud needs me. Gettin' close to dinnertime, you know." She winked at Kaleb before turning her attention back to Grace. "I hope you enjoy your stay with us. Just let me know if there's anything I can do for you."

Luann hugged both of them before hurrying back to her golf cart. "Catch ya later." She waved as she sped off.

Kaleb looked at Grace and they both cracked up.

"You won't find many people with a bigger heart than Luann," he said.

Grace lifted a shoulder. "According to her, you'll give her a pretty good run for her money."

"Yeah, well. She tends to exaggerate." He toed at the dirt. "Hey, look, about the tire. I'm sorry if I was a little pushy."

"A little?" There went that perfectly arched brow again.

"Okay, so one of the first things you should probably know about me is that I like to be in control."

Her gaze narrowed. "Does that mean you'll constantly be looking over my shoulder at work? Questioning my abilities?"

"Not at all. Your job entails things I won't even pretend to know about. But I do appreciate an attention to detail and, based on our earlier conversations, I think you bring that to the table."

She nodded, her lips pursed. "And just so you'll know, I'm…not usually so stubborn. My mother taught me to play well with others."

He chuckled.

"Speaking of my mother, can you tell me how to get to Fifth Street?"

"Sure." He pointed toward the southeast corner of town. "Simply head up Seventh Avenue and make a right onto

Fifth." He faced her again. "Donna and Roger will be happy to see you."

Her smile evaporated, her eyes narrowing. "How do you know who my mother is?"

His stomach muscles tightened. She didn't know. "Uh, Roger. He's one of my guides. Matter of fact, he's the one who convinced me I should buy Mountain View Tours." Even going so far as to provide some financial backing. But she didn't need to know that. Nor did she need to know that, after learning Grace was one of the applicants for the office-manager position, Roger was the one who'd recommended her for the job.

"One of your guides?"

"I'm surprised they didn't say anything to you."

"I'm not." The words were mumbled, so he wasn't sure he heard her correctly.

"What?"

"I mean, they probably thought I already knew." She shifted the compressor to her other hand and proceeded to unroll the electrical cord. "So, it looks like Roger and I will be working together, huh?"

"To a point, yeah. I mean, he's a guide, so it's not like he'll be hanging around the office all day or anything." Lowering his head, he tried to read her expression. "That's not going to be a problem, is it?"

She continued with the cord, seemingly taking forever. When her eyes finally met his, her smile appeared a little too forced. "No. No problem at all."

Then why did he suddenly get the feeling it was going to be a big problem?

With her tire fixed and Kaleb gone, Grace swapped her traveling clothes for a pair of skinny jeans and a long-sleeved tunic top and grabbed a quick bite to eat before heading to her mother's. She hadn't planned to visit until tomorrow evening. However, after learning that Roger worked for Kaleb, she decided she'd better put in an appearance tonight or else face the possibility of an even more awkward scene tomorrow at work.

Why hadn't Mama said something—anything—when Grace told her where she'd be working? Instead, her email said simply, Can't wait to see you.

Now, as Grace plodded up Seventh Avenue, hesitation plagued each step, her roast beef sandwich souring in her stomach. She and her mother had never had the kind of close relationship Grace had shared with her father. No, while her mother and Lucy bonded over clothes and shoes, Grace and her father bonded over motorcycles.

Then, suddenly, Daddy was gone and Mama married someone else. Leaving Grace drifting aimlessly, without a compass or anything to hold on to. Not even her husband.

Seemed she didn't fit in anywhere.

Turning onto Fifth Street, she continued a couple more blocks. Moving past the rows of mostly older homes, some well kept, some not so much, she could feel the weight of anxiety settling in her chest. Then she spotted the slate-blue-and-white Queen Anne style two-story.

Her heart pounded against her rib cage. How could she do this? Set foot inside *his* house? Not her mother's, not one they'd purchased together, but the house Roger had grown up in, according to her mother.

You're simply going to visit your mother.

She drew in a deep breath. That was right. Maybe he wouldn't even be there. She eyed the white wicker chairs and love seat on the porch. Perhaps she wouldn't even have to go inside.

Picking up the pace, she marched up the front walk, climbed the two white wooden steps and rang the doorbell.

A minute later, the door swung open, and Roger stood before her. His silver hair still had that tousled appearance, and the medium blue Henley he wore seemed to match the color of his eyes. If he were anyone else, she'd think him a fairly handsome man.

"Grace!" Though his smile was quick, his brow puckered in confusion as he pushed open the screen door. "We weren't expecting you until tomorrow. Come on in."

The aroma of lavender and vanilla wafted outside, stirring fond memories of every military house Grace had ever lived in. No matter where in the world they were, Mama's favorite fragrance made it feel like home.

Shaking off the recollection, she kept her feet planted on the porch. "Um…is my mother here?"

"'Fraid not. They're having a VBS planning meeting at the church tonight."

Of course, her mother would be there. She had taken an active role in every vacation Bible school at every church they'd ever attended.

Apparently her love for Grace's father was the only thing that didn't transcend time.

Roger held the door wider. "You're welcome to come in and wait on her, though."

"No. Thank you." Grace squared her shoulders. "I hear you're a guide at Mountain View Tours."

"Going into my fourth year."

She nodded. "And nobody felt the need to share this information with me?"

He moved out onto the porch in his white sock feet. "We weren't trying to deceive you, Grace. We were afraid that if you knew I worked there, too, you might not come. Your mother's looking forward to seeing you."

Looking everywhere but at Roger—the wooden floorboards, the neighbor's house, the hanging flower basket swaying in the breeze—Grace fought to keep her breathing even as the words seeped in. While her knee-jerk reaction was to reject the notion, she knew deep inside that Roger was probably right.

"In that case—" she started down the steps "—I guess I'll see you around. Tell my mother I stopped by."

"I'll do that. And, Grace?"

As much as she hated to, she halted her retreat and turned.

"You're welcome here anytime." His smile was sincere, the lines around his eyes indicating it was something he did a lot.

Maybe Lucy was right. Maybe he wasn't so bad. But Grace wouldn't betray her father.

Her gaze drifted to the ground before bouncing back to Roger. "Good night."

She moved down the street at a much faster pace than when she'd arrived, ready to put this day behind her. Despite her long sleeves, the cool evening air sent chill bumps skittering down her arms, making her wish she'd brought her jacket. All she wanted to do now was get back to her camp, crawl into bed and hope tomorrow wasn't as convoluted as today.

Coming to Ouray was supposed to rejuvenate her. Instead, it felt more like a chore. That cruise ship was sounding better and better all the time.

Rubbing her arms, she surveyed the surrounding mountains. Though the town lay bathed in shadows, the sun's fading rays radiated from behind the western slope. Glancing eastward, her breath caught in her throat. The gray, volcanic-looking mountains that seemed to hug the town were now painted the most beautiful, yet indescribable color. Shades of orange, rose and yellow blended into one harmonious hue that was unlike anything she'd ever seen before.

"Grace?"

Turning, she saw Kaleb coming up the block. Couldn't she go anywhere in this town without running into him?

Gravel crunched beneath each step as he continued toward her, looking annoyingly handsome. "Enjoying the alpenglow?"

"The what?"

Hands on his hips, he nodded in the direction of the colorful mountain. "Alpenglow. It's a phenomenon that often happens this time of night."

She readily focused on nature's beauty. "What causes it?"

He shrugged. "Something about the sun reflecting off particles in the atmosphere. I tend not to question it. I simply enjoy it."

"I can see why." It had that same captivating quality as a rainbow. A supernatural splendor that commanded one's attention.

"Were you visiting your mom?"

The colors had begun to fade by the time she faced Kaleb. "That was my intention, but she wasn't home. Roger said something about a vacation Bible school meeting."

"Yeah, that was tonight." He dragged the toe of his work boot over the dirt road. "Did you and Roger have a nice visit?"

Visit? They barely conversed. But getting the impression that Kaleb was rather fond of Roger, she said, "I suppose. Yeah."

"He's a good man. A fellow vet, too. But then, I suppose you already knew that."

She did not, but was too exhausted to offer anything more than a nod.

"Hey, I hate to cut this short, but I need to get back to camp. New job tomorrow." She had to make herself smile. "Gotta get a good night's rest so I can make a good impression on my boss."

"I don't think that'll be a problem." His grin set off a strange and unwanted fluttering in her midsection. "Don't forget to make sure any food you've got at your campsite is secured inside a cooler or something with a latch. Bears like to wander down the mountain at night and help themselves."

She puffed out a laugh. "You're kidding, right?"

His smile evaporated. "Not at all. I'm surprised Bud didn't say something to you when you checked in."

The fluttering morphed into a whirlwind. "Let me get this straight. While I'm asleep, bears are going to be roaming around my campsite?"

"Possibly."

She surveyed the rapidly darkening sky, sweat suddenly beading her brow. "I'll see you tomorrow." Despite the fatigue nipping at her heels, she broke into a jog.

Controlling bosses, working with her stepfather and now bears. With all that on her mind, she'd never get any sleep.

At this rate, Ouray was turning out to be the worst idea her sister ever had.

Chapter Three

Kaleb pulled his Jeep into a parking spot alongside Mountain View Tours shortly after noon the next day. As promised, he'd taken Grace on her first tour to Yankee Boy Basin and, so far, it had been a fantastic day. "My goal is to create a memorable experience for each of our guests. One they'll talk about for the rest of their lives."

And judging by Grace's reaction, he'd achieved just that. The look of unequivocal reverence as she took in the snow-covered peaks that stretched as far as the eye could see was something he'd never forget. Her genuine interest and appreciation for every little thing, from the old mines to the cascading waterfalls to a grosbeak's sweet song, reinforced his belief that he'd made the right decision in hiring her.

Now he shifted the vehicle into Park, glancing toward her in the passenger seat. "Unfortunately, the previous owner didn't feel the same way, so I've got an uphill battle."

"Which is why we need to appeal to folks from the moment they walk into Mountain View Tours, if not before." She gathered her things and exited the vehicle.

He climbed out, liking the way she used the word *we*, as if they were one, focused on the same common goal. Yes, the sooner he could bring Grace up to speed and put her to work, the better off his business would be. Memorial weekend, the unofficial kickoff of the high season, was only a few weeks away, and there was still much to do.

Meeting her at the front of the Jeep, he stared down at her. "And how do we do that?"

"I have a few ideas, though you may not like them." She wasn't afraid to meet his gaze. As though issuing a challenge.

Like he'd back down from a challenge. "Try me."

"Okay. You said you want to create a memorable experience for your guests."

"Yes."

"What if we added a tagline?" She shifted her weight from one foot to the next. "Something like, 'Mountain View Tours... Memories in the making.'"

He let the phrase tumble through his brain. "Okay. Yeah. I'm kinda liking that. Tells people exactly what our goal is."

"Just like a tagline is supposed to."

"That would look good on my new brochures, too." Rubbing his chin, he took a step back. "Which reminds me. You wouldn't happen to know anything about designing brochures, would you?"

"Sure. I'm pretty good with websites, too."

He couldn't stop smiling. "Grace, you may just be the best thing that ever happened to Mountain View Tours. So what other suggestions have you got?"

Clasping her notepad and camera against her chest, she took a deep breath. "I think you need to consider sprucing up the front office. Something as simple as a fresh coat of—"

"No."

"Why no—"

"We discussed this yesterday. The rustic look stays."

She took a step closer, her gaze narrowing. "For your

information, it's industrial, not rustic. And it only works if it's done right." She pointed toward the building. "That's not it."

Hands on his hips, he put himself toe-to-toe with her. "So what? My building, my business, my decor."

After a momentary staredown, she took a step back. "You asked for my input."

Something he'd think twice about next time.

Exasperation mounting, he started toward the building and pushed through the front door, the heels of his work boots hammering against the concrete floor. "Sami, would you please tell Grace the office looks perfectly fine."

Sami glanced up from behind the counter. "Grace, the office looks perfectly fine. *If* you like drab and uninviting."

Behind him, Grace choked back a laugh.

He glared at his sister.

"I'm serious, Kaleb." Sami rounded the counter. "This place is about as lackluster as you can get. I about fell asleep while you were gone. You need to liven things up. Make Mountain View Tours a place people *want* to be."

"Now, where have I heard that before?" Tapping a finger to her lips, Grace pretended not to look at him. A move that only served to further annoy him.

Sami stepped between them, her dark brown gaze fixed on Kaleb. "Mom and I were talking about this just a little while ago. You know that we all want Mountain View Tours to be a success. However, we also know that you have some huge hurdles to overcome."

He couldn't argue with her so far. No matter how much he might want to.

"Which means you need to do whatever you can to overcome some of those hurdles."

"Like replacing all of the tour trucks and rental fleet? I've already done that."

Sami jammed a fist into her hip. "That's not what I'm talking about." She strode to the counter, spread out a swath of papers then stabbed them with her finger. "This is what I'm talking about. Just look at these before and after photos I found online."

He didn't want to look at them. But curiosity got the best of him.

Easing toward the desk, he cast his sister a wary eye. "Those are some pretty dramatic changes." Not to mention costly.

"Yep. All with little more than paint."

Grace sidled up beside Sami, no doubt pleased to have someone else in her corner. "I like how they incorporated the brick wall into the design of this one." She pointed from the picture to the brick wall behind his reception counter. "With the right color paint, some rustic elements, you could really make that stand out."

"Though they don't look like much right now, Kaleb's got some great pieces around here he could use." Sami turned. "Like that old Coke machine." She pointed across the room. "That thing is too cool to be hidden in a corner."

Grace strolled over to the vintage machine. "It's not often you find a soda machine that offers glass bottles. Does it work?"

"Yes," said Kaleb.

"Sami's right, then." She faced them again. "You need to move this someplace more prominent. Keep it stocked and you've got another source of income."

Kaleb tried to hide his annoyance. Not only due to the bossy women in front of him, but the fact that he hadn't given more consideration to the Coke machine.

"So what do you say, Kaleb?" Sami looked like a kid begging to open just one gift before Christmas. "We're only talking about the cost of materials. Mom and I are both willing to paint."

"Me, too." Grace thrust her arm in the air like a second grader. "It'd be fun. As a matter of fact—" She waved a hand then dropped it to her side. "Ah, never mind." Her narrowed gaze drifted to Kaleb. "I've learned to keep my suggestions to myself."

"Oh, no. You're not getting off that easy." Sami inched toward her. "Out with it, Grace."

Grace looked from him to Sami, as if deliberating whether or not to divulge her secret. "What if you had a grand opening? Something that invited people to come in and check out the new Mountain View Tours."

Sami's eyes grew wide. "That's an outstanding idea." She whirled toward Kaleb. "We could do it Memorial Day weekend. You could have your new trucks on display, offer discounts on tours… We could have cookies, balloons—"

He held up a palm, cutting off his sister. "No. I appreciate the suggestion. However, something like that involves a lot of work. I think we best focus our energies on bringing in business."

"That's exactly what we're trying to do." Returning her fist to her hip, Sami scowled at him. "Besides, wasn't it just the other day I heard you say that you were looking for a way to separate the new Mountain View Tours from the old?"

He hated it when she used his own words against him. "Yes. But a party wasn't exactly what I had in mind."

"Then what did you have in mind?" His sister's smug grin only served to irritate him.

He didn't have a response. All he knew was that painting and parties took time. Time that he didn't have.

"Kaleb," Sami continued, "you've said a million times

how important this first season is going to be. Why not do it right?"

Grace cleared her throat. "All you'd really have to do for a grand opening is set up shop outside. Go to the people instead of waiting for them to come to you." She tucked a strand of dark hair behind her ear. "We're talking very little time and effort. However, the payoff could be worth it."

His sister's expression softened. "So what do you say, big brother? You going to go big or go home?"

He definitely didn't want to go home. Not only would he be letting his investors down, he'd be lost. He'd been working toward this goal for years.

Scanning the bare-bones office, he could see where it might seem a little cold.

We need to appeal to folks from the moment they walk into Mountain View Tours, if not before.

Of course, the more appealing things were, the more likely people were to be drawn in.

He eyed his sister. "You and Mom will do all the work?"

"And Grace." Hope lit Sami's dark eyes. "When she's not doing things for you, that is."

"And you'll get the work done quickly?"

"As quick as we can. After all, Memorial Day is right around the corner."

He lowered his arms to his sides. Even though he was ready to say yes, he paused for effect. "Okay, you can re-decorate. So long as I approve all ideas and colors first. Got it?"

"Got it." Sami's grin was so big, he thought she might burst. "And what about the grand opening? Scott and I would be happy to help out. I'm sure Mom and Dad would, too."

Honestly, the more he thought about it, the more he

liked the idea. Though he didn't have to let his sister or Grace know.

"We can probably work something out."

"Yes!" Sami charged him then and hugged his neck so tight he could barely breathe. "Okay." Letting go, she began her retreat. "I'm going to run over to the hardware store to look at some paint chips." After a final scan of the place, she continued. "I can't wait." She yanked open the door. "Oh! Hello, Donna." She held the door for Grace's mother.

"Hello, Sami." The woman in her late fifties continued inside, looking as well dressed as ever in her tan slacks and flowing blue shirt. "Kaleb, I hope you don't mind me dropping by to see my daughter."

"Not at all." He could use a break. Being ganged up on by two headstrong women was enough to do any man in. "This'll give me a chance to run and pick us up some lunch before we get down to business."

"It's so good to see you." Donna embraced her daughter. Her short auburn hair was a contrast to Grace's long dark brown. However, they shared the same hazel eyes.

"Hi, Mama." Grace's hug seemed a bit more tentative. Even awkward.

Perhaps because he was there.

"Grace? Burger or sandwich?"

Her mother released her.

"Burger's fine. With everything, please."

"Done." He started for the door. "See you later, Donna." Outside, he crossed the street and headed toward Granny's Kitchen.

Scrubbing a hand over his face, he let go a sigh. Talk of redecorating and a grand opening, while both great ideas, also added to his angst. There was so much to do and so little time in which to do it. Could they really pull it off?

God, I want to get this right.

Honestly, he really liked the ideas Grace and Sami proposed. And if everything went according to plan...

On the flip side—

No. He wasn't going to go there. Because for as much as he hated to admit it, Grace just might be the key to his success.

Grace did not want to do this now.

She hadn't seen her mother since Lucy's wedding last year. Right after Grace had returned from deployment and learned that her own marriage was over. So why on earth would Mama come to Mountain View Tours—a public place—for their first encounter? What if the place had been filled with customers?

Unless her mother was trying to protect herself, thinking Grace wouldn't call her out if someone else was around. But now that Kaleb was gone...

"Why didn't you tell me Roger worked here?"

Mama squared her shoulders in a defiant manner.

"I'm not trying to pick a fight, Mama. The news just kind of blindsided me, that's all. I wish you would have told me."

Lifting her chin, her mother said, "If I had, though, would you have taken the job?"

"I guess we'll never know, will we?" Though resignation laced Grace's tone, she made sure there was no accusation.

"Grace, you're my daughter. I miss you. And I'd like to have a relationship with you."

"Like you do with Lucy." The two of them were always chatting up a storm about the latest fashion trends, celebrities and such. Things Grace didn't have a clue about. Especially after spending ten months at sea.

Mama shrugged. "It's easier with Lucy. She lets me in."

"I tell you things."

Her mother chuckled. "Only when I ask. Even then, you only give me enough to get me to stop with the questions. Yet you never had any problem talking to your father." Mama looked away. "I always envied that."

Envy? Seriously? Grace's gut churned with the shock of Mama's revelation, leaving any words she might have said stuck inside.

She glanced out the window. "Kaleb will be back soon." And she didn't know how to continue this conversation with her mother. "We've got a lot of work to do."

"See what I mean. Instead of allowing anyone in, you avoid whatever makes you uncomfortable."

She let Aaron in. And look how that turned out.

"This isn't about being uncomfortable. This is reality. And reality dictates that I have a job, which means I have a boss. A boss who will be back any moment, expecting me to work." She took a deep breath, contemplating her next offer. "I can stop by tonight…if you like."

Mama's expression turned hopeful. "For dinner? I'll make your favorite."

Grace's spirits lifted a notch. "Nonna Gigi's lasagna?"

"Of course."

Grace's mouth watered just thinking about it. Nonna Gigi's lasagna was the ultimate in comfort food. One Grace had not had the pleasure of indulging in for years.

Mama sure knew how to dangle the carrot.

"I don't get off work until six."

"That's all right. We typically don't eat until six thirty or seven."

"One burger with everything." Kaleb blew through the door. "Along with some of the freshest French fries in Ouray."

She caught a whiff of the enticing aroma as he walked past. If they tasted half as good as they smelled…

Her mother eased toward the door. "I'll get out of your hair so you two can get back to work."

Kaleb set the white paper bag on the counter and turned to face them. "Did Grace tell you we're going to be doing some redecorating in here?" He gestured his hand about the office.

"She did not." Mama paused, her hand on the doorknob, a smile at the corners of her mouth.

Evidently, now that he'd had time to think, Kaleb decided the suggestion had been a good one.

"Looks like we'll be doing some painting and who knows what else to get the place in shape."

"Oh, I'd love to help." Having transformed many a bland military house into a warm and inviting home, Mama not only loved, but had lots of experience with decorating.

Working alongside her, though?

Slinking toward the desk and the tantalizing aromas, Grace spotted the local newspaper on the corner of the counter.

"That'd be great, Donna. Like my grandmother always said, many hands make light work."

Try as she might, Grace couldn't share Kaleb's enthusiasm. Too many memories to be objective, she supposed.

"What's Roger up to today?"

"He's substitute teaching at the school."

Talk of Roger had Grace wishing she were already on that cruise ship. She picked up the newspaper and thumbed through the pages. Maybe there was another job in Ouray that she might enjoy. One that didn't involve working with her stepfather.

"Grace?"

"Hmm…?" She looked at Kaleb first, then her mother.

"I'll see you for dinner, then?"

She closed the paper. Folded it. "Just as soon as I get off work."

With her mother gone, Kaleb opened the bags and sorted out the food.

Grace accepted her burger. "Sorry my mother interrupted us like that. I'm sure she won't make a habit of dropping in."

"Don't worry about it. After missing you last night, she was probably eager to see you. I understand." He passed her a small bag of fries. Thin-cut, just the way she liked them. "Pull up a stool." He pointed behind the desk.

While he unwrapped his burger and took a bite, she grabbed the basic wooden stool and sat down, her appetite waning.

"Something wrong with your burger?"

"No. Just thinking about this evening."

Kaleb jerked his head up, a blob of mayo clinging to his bottom lip. "Problem?"

He grabbed a napkin and wiped his mouth.

She picked up a fry, rolling it between her forefinger and thumb. "I just don't know how I'm going to handle spending an entire evening with Roger."

"Why? He's a great guy."

"So people keep telling me. But what kind of guy goes after a woman whose husband has been dead less than a year?"

Kaleb settled his sandwich on top of the flattened bag. "Did you know Roger lost his wife to cancer, too?"

"I knew he was married." But beyond that...

"For thirty-five years." Kaleb wiped his hands. "Everyone around here worried about him after Camille died. My mom said he looked like a dead man walking. Until he met your mother."

Grace tossed the fry she'd been holding back into the bag. "Sometimes life really stinks."

"Yep. The buffet line of life is notorious for throwing stuff on our plates that we don't necessarily like." He shrugged. "Doesn't mean they're not good for us, though. What doesn't kill us makes us stronger, right?"

Staring at her handsome boss, who seemed to have the world at his feet, she puffed out a disbelieving laugh. "What could you possibly know about it?"

He narrowed his gaze on her, as though contemplating his response. "Far more than you might think." He rounded the counter then, his expression intense, and lifted the left leg of his cargo pants.

"What are you—" At the sight of his prosthetic leg, her words and her heart skidded to a halt. "Oh, my." She continued to look at the metal-and-hard-plastic contraption that went all the way above his knee. "I—I never would have guessed."

She looked at him now. "What—"

"IED. Cost me four of my buddies and my leg." He let the pant leg drop. "So don't go acting like you're the only one who's been handed a raw deal. Because, sweetheart, I do know a little something about it."

Chapter Four

Grace would love nothing more than to go back to her campsite and lick her wounds. Next time, she needed to think twice before inviting someone else to her pity party.

In one swift, stealthy strike, her boss had put an end to her sulking. And yes, despite her strong desire to turn tail and run, Kaleb was still her boss. Despite their disagreements, she felt as though she could make a difference at Mountain View Tours.

Of course, that also meant she'd still be working with Roger, so she supposed she should put aside her preconceived notions and, at least, give the guy a chance.

Now here she stood in Mama and Roger's cottage-style kitchen, feeling like a bit of a jerk. She hadn't realized he'd lost his wife of thirty-five years. Probably because she never took the time to listen to anything her mother—or anyone else—had to say about him.

"What can I do to help, Mama?" She pushed up the long sleeves of her purple T-shirt and headed toward the farmhouse sink under the window to wash her hands.

"Why don't you set the table while I finish with this salad." Her mother rested the knife on the marble-topped island and wiped her hands on a dish towel before open-ing one of the white cupboards behind her.

"Silverware?"

"First drawer on the right." Mama pointed with her elbow while pulling out a stack of plates. She set them on the counter. "We'll eat in the dining room tonight."

"Okay." Eating utensils clasped in one hand, Grace reached for plain white plates with her other. "I think you gave me one too many."

"No, I didn't. The fourth one is for Kaleb. Roger thought it would be nice to invite him for dinner, too."

Grace simply stood there, uncertain what to make of her mother's sudden announcement. After all the head-butting she and Kaleb had done today.

"Oh, and place mats and napkins are in the drawer in the hutch." Mama picked up her knife and continued slic-ing tomatoes. "Let's go with the turquoise ones. Add a little color."

Good thing Grace's workday had ended on a positive note. Otherwise, seeing Kaleb tonight could prove to be even more awkward.

She moved into the dining room and set the plates and silverware on the table before searching for the linens. Not that it would be difficult. Mama always kept them in the right-hand drawer.

Turning toward the wall at the far end of the room, she vaguely recognized the tall piece of furniture whose glass case held Mama's collection of pastel-colored Depression glass. The style of the piece was similar to the one Grace remembered growing up, except instead of the honey oak finish, this one was white.

She pulled the crystal knob to open the drawer on the right and gasped. It *was* the same piece. While the out-side of the hutch had been painted, the inside of the drawer still bore hers and Lucy's names. Names they'd written in permanent marker along the inside of the drawer. A move that had earned them both a stern scolding and a lengthy time-out.

Stepping back, she stared at the furniture piece, a bittersweet feeling leaching into her heart. She remembered the look of pure delight on her mother's face the Christmas Daddy presented it to her. "You need a special place to display your collection," he'd told her.

Grace thought it was the most beautiful, if not ginormous, thing she'd ever seen. Yet as she stared at it now, the hutch looked prettier than ever. Like a better version of itself.

A noise in the kitchen interrupted her reverie and stole her attention.

"Smells delicious." Roger closed the door behind him, wiping his booted feet on the rug before making his way into the room. His arm snaked around her mother's waist as he set a plastic grocery sack on the counter. He said something, though the words were too soft for Grace to hear. Whatever it was, though, made her mother giggle and had a blush creeping into her cheeks.

"Love words" were what she and Lucy used to call it when Daddy would whisper sweet nothings into Mama's ear. Sometimes she would blush, sometimes not, but either way, Grace and Lucy knew it was an intimate conversation, meant only for Mama and Daddy.

Suddenly uncomfortable, Grace grabbed the place mats and napkins and returned her focus to the table.

"Hello, Grace." Roger stood just on the other side of the doorway between the two rooms. "Glad you could make it." Hands stuffed into the pockets of his jeans, he seemed to look everywhere but at her.

Just like she did when she was uncomfortable.

Could it be that Roger was as nervous about tonight as she was?

"Thank you for having me." Hands shaking, she finished laying out the silverware, realizing she'd forgotten to grab another set. "You have a lovely home."

"Yeah." He moved closer, just enough to admire the dining room and adjoining living room. Both had that same cottage feel, lots of white furniture against dark hardwood floors and pale blue-gray walls. "Your mother's quite the decorator."

He'd let her mother redecorate? But this was his house.

"She managed to fuse our former lives and our new life into something fresh and different."

Much like the old hutch.

All of Lucy's words about Roger being a good guy flooded her memory. Grace had chosen to ignore her sister. Now her emotions warred within.

Perhaps her mother wasn't quite so eager to forget the past after all.

The doorbell rang then.

"That would be Kaleb." Moving along the opposite side of the table, Roger headed toward the door.

Feeling as though she still had egg on her face when it came to her boss, Grace took the opportunity to retrieve that fourth set of utensils.

Inside the kitchen, her mother was removing a large baking dish from the oven. The aromas of meat, cheeses and whatever other secret ingredients made up Nonna Gigi's famous lasagna wafted throughout the room, reminding Grace of simpler times.

She inhaled deeply, wishing she could find a way to capture the scent for those times when life got rough. "That smells amazing."

"Always does." Mama set the pan atop the stainless-steel stove, then grabbed a sheet pan that held a split loaf of French bread spread with garlic butter and sprinkled with cheese. "Now all I have to do is get this garlic bread baked." She set the pan in the oven and adjusted the heat.

Hearing Kaleb's voice in the other room, Grace opened the drawer and took out another knife, fork and spoon. "Mama?"

"Yes, baby." Leaning her hip against the island, she gave Grace her full attention.

Grace pushed the drawer closed. "Did you know Kaleb was injured in the army?" His revelation had stunned, if not shamed, her. Sure she'd noticed that something was a little off in his gait on occasion, but she thought maybe he had a bad knee. Boy, was she wrong.

"Oh, yes. He doesn't hide it. In fact, he's an inspiration to everyone here, sharing his story at area schools and churches. He's our own real-life hero."

A hero whose title had come at a great price. Yet he didn't seem bitter or angry, and she wondered how that could be.

"Good evening, ladies."

Both Grace and her mother turned at the sound of Kaleb's deep voice.

"Hello there, Kaleb." Mama tossed her potholders on the island. "We're so happy you could join us."

"Are you kidding? After hearing Grace talk about her grandmother's lasagna all afternoon, I was thrilled when Roger extended the invitation."

His attention shifted to Grace then, his smile reaching across the room, wrapping around her heart like a warm blanket on a cold night.

She couldn't help noticing that while she'd come directly from work, he'd changed into a pair of dark wash jeans and a tailored red-and-white button-down that hugged his muscular torso. His hair was also damp, indicating he'd likely showered.

Nothing like being shown up by a guy. Especially one who'd suddenly garnered a great deal of her respect.

Making dinner with Mama and Roger seem like a cake-walk compared to spending the evening with a guy whose character and outlook on life had her taking a long, hard look at herself...and not liking what she saw.

Kaleb had hoped for a relaxing evening and, so far, it had been just that. While there was no question that he wanted to support Roger by being here for him, he feared things could be a little tense. After the way he shut Grace down today... And even though they'd patched things up, one never knew how well that patch might hold.

Sitting in Roger and Donna's dining room, next to Grace, no less, Kaleb finished his last bite of lasagna. "Donna, your grandmother's lasagna has a new fan." He set his fork atop his empty plate. "I've never tasted anything like it." It was the perfect balance of meat, cheese and pasta. And those seasonings. Just the right kick, without overpowering the other flavors.

Grace's mother dabbed the corners of her mouth with her cloth napkin. "That's the response this recipe usually gets."

"I only wish she'd make it more often." Roger nudged his wife's elbow with his own, sending her a playful grin.

Donna blushed, returning her napkin to her lap. "Kaleb, I can't tell you how excited I am about the Hometown Heroes exhibit at the museum."

His chest tightened. The way it always did when his name and the word *hero* were used in the same sentence. He was no hero.

"Hometown heroes? Museum?" Grace spooned another

small portion of lasagna onto her plate. Her third helping, if he wasn't mistaken. Where did she put it?

Donna addressed her daughter. "I volunteer at the historical museum here in town. We're planning to have a whole room dedicated to those men and women from Ouray who have served our country. We've received a few items— everything from photos to uniforms to ration cards—dating back to the First and Second World Wars, the Korean War and Vietnam." She smiled at Kaleb. "However, our most recent hero is going to round things out for us. Make the exhibit more personal and real by bringing it into the twenty-first century."

Eager to deflect the unwanted attention, Kaleb motioned toward Roger. "What about Roger? I'm sure he's got lots of items."

"Are you kidding?" Roger draped an arm across the back of his wife's chair. "Donna had me pulling boxes from my Vietnam days out of the attic weeks ago."

"We'll have the ribbon cutting on June twenty-third, a day we're calling Hometown Heroes Day, and Kaleb here has volunteered to give a short speech, along with our other donors."

Volunteered? More like coerced. A bunch of women ganging up on him like that, plying him with all kinds of baked goods. A fellow didn't stand a chance.

Now he was committed.

"When do you think you'll have your items ready for us?" Donna smiled sweetly.

"I need to finish sorting through everything." Of course, before he could finish, he needed to actually start the process. For now, the untouched boxes were still stacked in one of his spare bedrooms, right where his parents had left them a month ago. He knew he needed to move a lever. Yet every time he thought about it, a sense of dread seemed to settle over him. "It's a little overwhelming."

"I can imagine." Leaning back, Donna folded her hands in her lap. "You were in the army how many years?"

"Eight."

Grace rested her elbow on the table, perched her chin on her palm and stared at him. "How many tours of duty?"

"Three. All in the Middle East."

Donna gasped. "I just had an idea."

Kaleb and Grace collectively turned to her mother.

"Grace, why don't you help Kaleb sort through his things?"

A look of horror flashed across Grace's face. She straightened, lowering her arm. "Mama, I don't think that's really appropriate. There may be some things that Kaleb doesn't want anyone else to see."

Donna laid a hand at the base of her neck. "Yes, I suppose you're right." She met Kaleb's gaze. "I apologize if I was out of line, Kaleb."

"No worries, Donna."

"Well, so long as we have everything by June ninth, we should be okay." Donna pushed away from the table. "Who's interested in dessert?"

Despite his stomach being twisted in knots with guilt, Kaleb managed to down a slice of chocolate cake, another of Grace's purported favorites, before bidding Roger and Donna farewell.

"I'm going to say good-night, too." Grace grabbed her jacket and pack from the closet near the front door. "Thank you for dinner, Mama." She hugged her mother, the gesture appearing more heartfelt than the one they'd shared earlier that day. "The lasagna was even better than I remembered."

Outside, the last vestiges of daylight faded in the western sky. The night air was cool, something he was used to, but he was glad Grace had a jacket.

They strolled along Fifth Street, silent. Was she feeling as sheepish in the wake of this afternoon's events as he was? He struggled to think of something to say, but couldn't.

Finally, "I, uh—" Grace stepped into the void. "I'm sorry for what my mother said. About me helping you. Obviously she's a little out of touch."

"Ah, she's harmless. I know there was no ill intent."

After another pause, Grace continued. "You haven't begun to sort through your stuff, have you?"

Wow. He wasn't expecting that. "You figured that out, huh?"

"Yep." Her gaze remained straight ahead.

For some odd reason, he felt relieved. As if his secret was finally out in the open. "I have every intention of meeting that deadline, you know."

"I know." Hands stuffed in the pockets of her jacket, she forged on. "But delving into your past makes you uneasy."

"How did you know?" He'd known this woman barely twenty-four hours and yet she was able to read him so well.

She shrugged. "We all have pasts."

He followed her around the corner at Seventh Avenue. "It's not like I'm hiding anything."

"I understand. You'd just prefer the past remain in the past."

"Sort of. It's just—"

She stopped in the middle of the street. Looked at him with eyes that seemed to cut right through him. "Just what?"

"Um— My prosthetic. Challenges. You know." Now it was his turn to shrug.

"Memories."

One innocuous word but, boy, did it pack a punch. "Yeah."

Her weak smile said she understood. "They have a way of sneaking up on us, don't they?"

Us? What memories did Grace not want to unearth?

"I can't imagine what you've gone through, Kaleb. But your sacrifice deserves to be honored. People *want* to honor it. Why not let them?"

Because they might see that I'm a fraud. That I'm not worthy of their honor.

They crossed Main Street, the sound of the river growing louder as they approached. Much like the turmoil cutting a swath through him. Why couldn't he go through those boxes? What was he so afraid of?

Perhaps Grace's mother was right. Maybe he did need help. Someone to give him direction and keep him on task. After all, he had a deadline and he was a man of his word.

But who would he ask? His mother would want him to donate everything. His father was too close to the situation, too. Maybe Roger. He was military and knew how to cut to the chase. Though Kaleb hated to take him away from Donna.

Why his gaze drifted to the woman walking beside him was beyond comprehension. He barely knew her. Still, she was military. So, in a practical sense, she would know what might be best for the museum. And, now that he thought about it, not having any personal attachment to him or anyone else might actually make her the best person for the job.

But there was a lot of stuff in those boxes. Stuff that spanned his life from boyhood to manhood. Did he really want her sifting through every photo and newspaper article? From basic training to the IED that ended his career.

They rounded onto Oak Street and Kaleb realized they were almost to the RV park. He'd been so lost in thought that he not only lost track of time, but location, as well. He hadn't intended to walk Grace home, though he supposed it was the gentlemanly thing to do.

Unfortunately, he didn't believe in accidents. God wanted him to walk Grace home for a reason. And as he continued to ponder the boxes in his spare room, he had a pretty good idea what that reason was.

"Grace?" He stopped in front of the empty campsite just down from hers and turned to look at her. "Would you be interested in helping me dig through my military memorabilia? I realize I'm asking a lot—I mean, you barely even know me—but I need help."

She watched him, seemingly intrigued. "How much stuff are we talking about?"

"At least a dozen boxes."

Her eyes widened. "No wonder you're overwhelmed."

He lifted a shoulder. "My mom insisted I share everything with her, and since I didn't know what was important and what wasn't, I had an ongoing box that I'd toss stuff into. When one got full, I'd send it to her and start on another."

Grace smiled then. "That's actually pretty sweet. Not many guys would be that considerate."

"You obviously haven't met my mother."

Grace snickered.

"So what do you say, Grace? Would you be willing to forfeit your free time to help a poor soul?"

"Give up my free time? Boy, you really know how to sell this."

"What if I throw in dinner?"

"Okay, now you're speaking my language." She crossed her arms over her chest, her gaze narrowing. "So why do you want me to help you?"

He stuffed his hands into the pockets of his jeans. "I don't know. I guess for the same reasons I hired you as my office manager. Military background, attention to detail…"

She nodded, yet remained silent for a moment. "Okay,

I'll do it." Lowering her arms, she turned and took two steps toward her campsite before twisting back around. "And just so you'll know, steak is my favorite meal."

Chapter Five

Grace wandered up Seventh Avenue three days later, surprised at how quickly Ouray had begun to take up residence in her heart, granting her a measure of tranquillity she hadn't known in a long time. She never would have thought the fabric of small-town life would feel so good. Yet here she was, savoring every cozy thread.

The laid-back lifestyle was a pleasant change. Much different from the navy. And the cruise ship would likely keep her hopping, too. Day and night. She'd better enjoy this while she had the chance.

Diet Dr Pepper in hand, she eased onto Fourth Street as the sun drifted farther below the town's western slope. After work, she'd gone back to her campsite and changed into a pair of sweatpants and a baggy sweater. If she was going to spend her evening weeding through a bunch of dusty boxes, she was going to be comfortable doing it.

She still wasn't sure why she'd agreed to help Kaleb sort through his army stuff. Didn't they spend enough time together at work? Or was Kaleb one of the reasons she was enjoying her time in Ouray?

Her steps slowed. That had to be the most ludicrous thought she'd ever had. She was about to embark on a high-seas adventure. See places she'd only dreamed of. The last thing she needed was a man in her life.

So why was her stomach fluttering at the sight of Kaleb's single-story bungalow?

Yellow with white trim and lots of gingerbread mill-work, the house beckoned passersby to pull up a rocking chair and enjoy life on its wraparound porch. Yet for as inviting as the house was, Grace found herself with a sudden case of nerves.

What was she? Sixteen again? She was there only to help him make a dent in those boxes.

With a bolstering breath, she downed the last of her drink, nudged her anxiety out of the way and continued up the walk onto the porch and rang the bell.

A few moments later, Kaleb appeared behind the screen door wearing the same medium wash jeans and work shirt she'd grown accustomed to seeing him in.

"You're just in time." He pushed the door open, inviting her inside.

"For what?" She slipped past him.

"I was just about to throw a couple of rib eyes on the grill."

Her mouth watered at the mention of steak. "But I thought we were going to—"

"You haven't eaten, have you?"

Following him toward the kitchen, she dared a few peeks at the rest of his house.

For as classic and feminine as the outside of Kaleb's house was, the inside was classically male. The living room had dark brown furniture positioned in front of a large flat-screen television and the dark wood coffee table was littered with game controllers and a laptop.

The next room had likely once been a dining room.

Sadly, it was now a gym, complete with a treadmill, weight bench and chin-up bar.

This lovely old home, victimized by a bachelor.

"No. But—"

"I figured, why settle for sandwiches when we could have steak."

But steak was an official meal. Like a— She gulped. A date.

That's what you get for telling him you like steak.

She had done that, hadn't she?

She cringed.

"How do you like yours cooked?" He tossed the words over his shoulder as they entered the kitchen.

"M-medium rare."

He snagged a plate with two thick slabs of meat from the kitchen counter and continued on to the back door. "Care to join me?"

"Sure." Tossing her empty can into the wastebasket as she passed, she followed him outside, admiring the small, though well maintained, backyard. "Anything I can do?"

The meat sizzled as he laid it atop the hot grates.

"Nope." He adjusted the steaks with a pair of tongs. "Baked potatoes are in the oven. Should be ready by the time the steaks are. I've got butter, sour cream, shredded cheese and bacon bits for those. Salad has already been tossed and is in the fridge."

Holy cow. In her world, that was a three-course dinner. "Sounds like you've been busy."

"Not really." He sent her a sheepish grin. "I used bagged salad."

She couldn't help smiling. "That's my favorite way to prepare it."

"I'm curious," he said as they delved into their meal twenty minutes later. "What are you planning to do come

September? When you're finished at Mountain View Tours?"

Sitting at a tiny round table tucked in the corner of the living room, she used her knife to slice off another bite of perfectly seasoned meat. "I'll be working as an excursions manager with Crowned Prince Cruise Lines."

He paused, his knife and fork in midair. "Seriously?"

She nodded, attacking her food. "The ship is in dry dock, undergoing renovations. My contract starts September fifteenth." She shrugged. "Hence the reason for temporary employment."

"You're not making this up, are you?" He watched her across the table.

"No." She paused her eating. "Why would I?"

He shook his head. "I've just never known anyone who's wanted to do that before."

"It's the same reason I joined the navy. The open seas. Exotic ports of call."

"But what about a home? Don't you want to settle somewhere?"

Her shoulders sagged. She'd tried that. It didn't work out.

Setting her utensils on her plate, she reached for her water, hoping to convey an air of confidence. "I prefer a more nomadic lifestyle. I mean, growing up, my parents were always moving here and there. It suits me."

He watched her curiously as she took a sip, but didn't say a word.

Uncomfortable with the sudden silence, she picked up her plate. "I think it's time we get started on those boxes."

After putting their dishes in the dishwasher, he led her down a short hallway to a small bedroom filled with boxes.

"This is my storage room."

"I can see that." Kaleb had more stuff in one room than she even owned. "Please tell me this isn't *all* memorabilia."

"No. Just these two stacks right here." He laid his hand atop the two that were just as tall as he was. Bankers boxes, no less. Not the small boxes she'd imagined he'd sent his mother.

"Kaleb, your mother is one blessed woman. But this is going to take us *forever.*"

"Now you understand my predicament." He lifted one from the top of the stack and set it on the floor. "Shall we?"

She dropped to her knees and blew out a breath. "We gotta start somewhere."

He lifted the lid. Inside were photos and newspaper articles. He picked up a picture. "This was from basic training." He studied the photo. Touched a finger to it. "Beau LeBlanc."

"What?" She leaned in for a closer look.

"Beau LeBlanc. He was my first friend at camp Benning. We were together every step of the way." Kaleb was silent a moment before clearing his throat. "All the way to the end."

Her heart twisted. No wonder Kaleb didn't want to go through these boxes. They were littered not only with memories, but painful ones at that. Memories he carried with him every single day in a very real way.

What should she do? Try to change the subject or let him remember?

Kaleb made the decision for her. "Beau was a Southerner to the core. Though not necessarily a gentleman. He had some spicy lingo, that one. Didn't take flak from no one." Kaleb looked at her without ever seeming to see her. "Then he met Vanessa and all that changed. I've never seen a guy mind his p's and q's as quickly as he did. He knew he'd hit pay dirt with her."

"Did they get married?"

"Just as soon as he could talk her into it." Kaleb's gaze fell to the worn hardwood floor. "Vanessa was pregnant when he was killed. Beau never got to see his little girl."

Grace's eyes fell closed. She would not cry in front of this man who was so grieved by the loss of his friends. Turning, she swiped away a couple of wayward tears before looking at Kaleb again.

"They're coming here, you know."

She watched him with curiosity. "Who?"

"The families. After I bought Mountain View Tours, Vanessa and one of the other wives thought it would be good to have a reunion here. So they're all coming to Ouray next month. Wives, kids, parents..."

"I can see that." Grace stretched her legs out in front of her. "They share a common bond."

"I just don't understand why they have to drag me into it." Kaleb stood, dropping the photo back into the box. "Perhaps we should do this another time." He held out a hand to help her up.

Allowing Kaleb to pull her to her feet, Grace was befuddled. Why wouldn't he want to see his friends' families? Their children? Didn't he realize he was their last connection to their loved ones?

She wished she knew the story surrounding the IED attack. But this definitely wasn't the time to ask. For now, she could only surmise that Kaleb was suffering from survivor's guilt.

"Whatever you think is best."

Perhaps next time, she'd suggest she go through the boxes alone and then bring any prospective museum items to him for approval. Seeing the pain swimming in Kaleb's suddenly dark eyes, though, she wondered if there would be a next time.

* * *

What was best was to leave the past in the past.

Kaleb had been a fool to think that having someone else with him would make this job any easier.

Standing in his spare room, staring down at Grace, he could only imagine what she must think of him. He recognized the pity in her gaze as she looked up at him. It was the same look his ex-fiancée, Gina, had as she sat with him at Walter Reed Medical Center.

Grace's pity was the last thing he wanted.

"I'll walk you home." He turned for the door.

"That's not necessary." She was on his heels as he started down the hall.

"Yes. It is." He tossed the words over his shoulder as they entered the living room. "It's dark outside." Besides, he needed the fresh air.

"I'm a big girl, Kaleb. I've walked alone in the dark before."

He jerked open the front door. "Yeah, well, not on my watch."

Outside, the night air was cooler than he'd expected. Just what he needed to clear his head and send those haunting memories back where they belonged.

"Thank you for dinner," said Grace as they started up the street. "That was the best steak I've had in a long time."

"You're welcome." The words came out harsher than he'd intended and he could sense Grace pulling away. She didn't deserve that. Not after she'd done so much to help him.

Touching her elbow, he stopped.

She followed suit.

"I appreciate your willingness to help me." He made sure to keep his words soft. "You've been nothing but great. Sorry I turned into such a jerk."

"No apology needed. However—" she shoved her hands into the pockets of her sweatpants "—if you'd like to talk about it, I've got a nice stack of wood just waiting for a campfire."

While steak might be Grace's weakness, campfires were his. The smell alone was the best aromatherapy ever. But she'd also thrown in the word *talk*. As if it was a stipulation. Nothing like driving a hard bargain.

"I may not be very forthcoming." He could at least be truthful.

Under the dim streetlamp, he saw something flicker in her eye. "We'll see about that."

"Is that a challenge?"

"Call it what you want." After a momentary staredown, she continued on, as though the gauntlet had been thrown down.

He walked beside her, uncertainty plaguing his every step. *Talk about it.*

Grace was practically a stranger. Why would she think he'd talk to her?

You're the one who asked her to help you go through your stuff.

Okay, so maybe Grace understood him better than most people. But only in terms of the military experience. Still, she hadn't suffered the loss of a comrade.

Arriving at her campsite, he spotted the stack of wood in question.

"So, what do you think?" She playfully eyed the small fire pit. "Seems like a nice night for a fire." She picked up a handful of kindling.

Surrounded by the sounds of the night, he studied the area. The camper. The canopy. The lone camp chair. "There's only seating for one."

Pursing her lips, she shook her head. "Nope. I've got a cooler that makes a great seat."

It was almost as though she were daring him to open up. In that case, "Bring it on."

The mischievous light in her eyes had him immediately rethinking things. Yet, before he knew it, an inferno threatened to overtake the tiny fire pit.

"Care for a drink? Water? Diet Dr Pepper?" With the pizzazz of a flight attendant, she smiled at him.

"No. I'm good." He picked up the lone camp chair and moved it from the canopy to the fire pit. For all practical purposes, they were alone. The nearest neighbor a large RV across the way.

He breathed in the aroma of fire and waited for calm to infuse his being. But it never came.

Grace settled beside him, atop the large cooler, a Diet Dr Pepper in hand. "Nice fire, huh?"

"Kinda small, if you ask me."

"Yeah, I'm a bit limited here. You should consider building a big fire pit in your backyard."

He glowered at her. "Maybe I will."

"Might come in handy." Her smug look teased him.

"Okay, what is it you want to know?" He wasn't afraid to call her bluff.

"I don't recall asking anything." She stared at the fire. "Though there's obviously something bothering you."

He leaned forward in his seat, rubbing his hands together. "And what do you think that something might be?"

"Why don't you tell me?" Her sideways glance only served to bug him more. But then, she already knew that.

"You're relentless, you know?"

She took a swig of her diet soda. "I have no idea what you're talking about."

He watched her a moment, his blood pressure rising.

He knew what she wanted. The question was, could he give it to her?

A part of him wanted to. The other part wanted to fight tooth and nail.

The odd thing was, he'd told his story to countless people, giving motivational speeches at area schools, churches and service organizations. Too many people had given up on themselves, on life and on God because they were too focused on what they didn't have. He wanted to encourage them to think about what they did have.

Yet talking with Grace about the event seemed, somehow, different. Back at the house, she'd got a glimpse of him at his worst. And he'd found himself on the receiving end of her pity.

He didn't want Grace's pity. He simply wanted her to know.

"Five years ago I was driving a Humvee and hit a trip wire." For as often as he'd shared his story, this time he found himself hesitating. He took a breath and forged ahead. "I don't remember much about the actual event. Just the sound of the explosion and then waking up in an army hospital several days later."

He shifted slightly, adjusting his artificial leg. "Of course, I had no idea what had happened. So my parents filled in the blanks the best they could." He looked over at Grace. "Seems the explosion packed enough punch to send that nine-thousand-pound vehicle flying through the air."

Her smile was a sad one.

"They explained that my jaw had been shattered, I'd been burned and that I'd lost my leg. And that my buddies…" He cleared the emotion that never failed to thicken his throat.

"I can't imagine how difficult that must have been." Illuminated by only the firelight, she twisted to face him. "But why do you blame yourself?"

"Who said that?"

"You did. Though not in so many words."

He searched her face, wondering how this woman could possibly read him so well. "What are you? Some kind of shrink?"

She puffed out a laugh. "Hardly. Just too curious for my own good."

The fire snapped and hissed, sending a shower of sparks into the air.

"Okay, then here you go. I don't like being called a hero and I don't need anybody's pity."

"Why would they pity you?"

"Why don't you tell me?"

Her gaze narrowed. "What are you getting at?"

"I saw the way you looked at me when I was talking about Beau. I don't need you to feel sorry for me, Grace."

"Feel sorry for you?" Setting her soda can down on the cooler, she stood. "I think you'd better get your eyes checked. The only thing I was feeling back there was your pain." She started to pace. "I can't even begin to comprehend the anguish you must feel over the loss of your friends. Or the torture you had to endure as you fought your way back from your injuries. I admire you. So to have you cheapen that by saying I feel sorry for you? I've got news for you, buddy. You're not worthy of my pity."

Chapter Six

Grace lay in her bed the next morning, listening to the rain slap against the waterproof fabric of the camper top, trying to decide who was the bigger fool. Kaleb for believing she felt sorry for him or her for going off on her boss. After all, the Kaleb of last night was not the same Kaleb she'd worked with all week. Last night's was a torn, grieving man, while the Kaleb that was her boss was one of the most positive and encouraging people she'd ever known.

No telling which one she'd face at work today. Assuming she still had a job, after the way she dismissed him last night.

She'd just have to apologize and prove herself worthy of her position with Mountain View Tours. Because there wasn't another job in town that paid as well. And she certainly wasn't going to spend the rest of the summer staying with her mother or Lucy.

Frustrated, she pulled the pillow from beneath her head, covered her face and screamed into the fluffiness.

There. That felt better.

She again tucked the pillow under her head and burrowed deeper under the covers, savoring a few more minutes of nothingness.

A drop of water landed on her cheek. Followed by another.

"What on earth..." She bounded off the bed that sat a couple of feet higher than the floor, eyeing her fabric roof. "Waterproof, my eye." Rubbing her bare arms, she spotted a leak in the ceiling. A tiny hole. Nothing some duct tape wouldn't fix.

She shivered as she opened the storage compartment beneath her mattress and rummaged through everything from extra blankets, to clothes, to her toolbox, but came up empty-handed. Turning her attention to the floor, she dropped to her knees and dug through her saddlebags.

"Where could that—" She snagged her gray navy sweatshirt and tugged it over her tank top as she stood. That was when she saw it.

Her breath. Clouding the frigid morning air.

In May? One should not be able to see their breath in the month of May. That was, unless they lived in Alaska.

Obviously, she'd spent too much time in warmer climates.

Her gaze inadvertently drifted heavenward and she huffed out a cloudy breath.

A few minutes later, she found the tape. It was indeed in her storage compartment, only inside her toolbox, which she'd failed to open the first go-round. By the time she patched the hole, the rain had stopped.

When she emerged from her tent a short time later, dressed in something warmer than her pajamas, gray clouds hovered over the town, obscuring the mountaintops. The air was still, yet damp and cold. She zipped up her jacket, annoyed that neither her sister nor her mother had warned her to bring some warmer clothes.

Fearful of more rain, she hauled a tarp from her storage compartment, along with some rope. Even with the hole patched, an extra layer of protection couldn't hurt. Might mean the difference between climbing into a wet bed or a dry one. Call her crazy, but she preferred her bedding dry.

Outside, she unfolded the blue plastic sheet and looped a rope through each corner. Then, standing on the tongue of the trailer, she attempted to throw one corner over the tent. At five foot seven, she wasn't exactly short, but since the tent peaked somewhere around seven feet, this was going to be a challenge.

"Looks like somebody could use a little help."

Grace jerked around at the sound of Kaleb's deep voice, the rubber sole of her riding boot slipping on the tongue's wet metal. She tried to catch herself, but fell backward, stumbling right into Kaleb.

"I gotcha."

Her heart broke into a thundering gallop as strong hands gently gripped her arms and lifted her straight. Warmth radiated from Kaleb's body, and she found herself longing to be enveloped in his embrace.

Shocked by the notion, she turned to face him, too embarrassed to look him in the eye. "What are you doing here?"

"Uh—hoping to ply you with a peace offering?" His brown insulated jacket looked a lot warmer than her leather number and she found herself coveting the black beanie pulled over his head and ears.

"What?" She pushed the hair out of her face, tucking it behind both ears.

"You had me awake half the night."

She felt both of her eyebrows reaching for the sky.

"Well, not *you*, but what you said."

Chagrin washed over her. She toed at the dirt with her boot. "Yeah, about that—"

"You were right."

Her gaze shot to his. "I was?"

"Yes. I owe you an apology for acting like a self-centered, misguided fool." He moved toward the picnic table. "And, since it's a cold morning, I thought I'd bring you hot coffee and breakfast to help win your forgiveness."

"Wait a minute." She scrubbed her hands over her face. "You have hot coffee?"

"Right here." He gestured to the cardboard carrier that held two cups. "I picked them up on my way over." He grabbed one and handed it to her. "Almost lost them when you fell, though."

"Well, I'm glad you didn't." She took hold of the cup, blessed heat seeping into her frozen fingers.

She took a sip, the hot liquid warming her from the inside out.

"There's some sugar and creamer in case you need it." He pointed to the cup holder.

"No, black is perfect."

"I had a feeling it might be."

She sent him a curious look.

"You were military. We learn to drink our coffee strong and black."

She puffed out a laugh and watched as it hung in the damp air. "And sometimes with chunks."

He nodded. "You won't have to worry about that today. Granny's Kitchen brews a decent cuppa joe, but without chunks." He reached behind him. "Celeste Purcell, the proprietor, also makes the best cinnamon rolls in town." He held up a white bag. "Get 'em while they're hot."

Grace couldn't help it. She simply stood there, blinking. A hot breakfast on this cold morning was more than she could have asked for. And far more than she would have managed on her own.

"Hello?" Kaleb waved the bag in her direction.

"Yes. Let's eat." She accepted a large, warm roll and a napkin and promptly picked off an icing-laden chunk. The sweet, gooey goodness practically melted in her mouth, filling her with a sugar-induced wave of delight. "This is *so* good."

"Does that mean I'm forgiven?"

Considering she had planned on apologizing to him... "Definitely."

Smiling, Kaleb eyed her tarp that now lay on the ground. "What were you trying to do up there?"

She held a hand in front of her mouth and spoke around her second bite. "There's a leak in my woof." She swallowed before continuing. "I patched it with duct tape, but looking at these clouds, I thought it might be a good idea to add an extra layer of protection."

"Do you have a heater in this thing?" He pointed to her camper.

Savoring another bite, she shook her head.

"Is that your only coat?"

She eyed her leather jacket. "Mmm-hmm."

Frowning, he said, "I'll be right back." He walked past her, gravel crunching beneath every booted step, and continued on to his Jeep, retrieved something from the backseat and returned. "It might be a little big, but it's warm." He handed her an insulated jacket, similar to the one he wore, only tan.

Grace was taken aback by the gesture. "Oh, I don't—"

"Yes, you do. Can. However, you were planning to object."

This was the Kaleb she'd experienced all week. The one who put others above himself. Suddenly she wondered if that wasn't what he was doing with his buddies who died. They were his heroes. And he'd let them down.

Which made the hero label people affixed to him feel as scratchy as woolen undergarments.

"Thank you." She spread the coat he gave her over her legs, humbled to realize that Kaleb hadn't just picked up coffee and breakfast. He'd actually put some thought into his actions.

It had been a long time since someone had anticipated her needs. Certainly no one on the ship. Even Aaron had grown accustomed to letting her take care of herself.

Hands perched low on his hips, Kaleb moved to the front of the trailer and studied her roof. Then he picked up the tarp and, with one strategic toss, sent it sailing. A few seconds later, the entire tarp covered her camper.

"You sure made that look easy." She stuffed the last bite of roll in her mouth and wiped her hands before hurrying to secure each corner with a stake.

"Height had its advantages."

He definitely had plenty of advantage, then.

"Everything secure?" He watched her as she finished hammering in the last stake.

"Yep." She approached him, hammer in hand, her stomach filled with that peculiar fluttering again. "Thank you for breakfast."

"My pleasure." He stared down at her, making her feel more petite than tall.

"I really should get ready for work."

"I'm sure your boss will understand if you're late."

Yes! She still had a job.

"Perhaps. But I'm not one to push the envelope."

He quirked a brow. "I don't know about that."

Her gaze lowered. "Yeah..."

Laying a finger to her chin, he tilted her head to look at him. "Thank you for holding me accountable."

Her mouth went dry. "I—uh..."

The corners of his mouth lifted. "What are you planning to work on today?"

"Well, I…" *The website, you idiot.* "The website. Now that the brochures are off to the printer, I'm hoping to finish the website."

"I'm still in awe of your talents, Grace." He dropped his hand and she found herself missing his touch. "Seems wherever I'm lacking, you know just how to pick up the slack." He turned and waved as he started for his Jeep. "See you at the office."

Grace watched him walk away, feeling a little disconcerted. For someone who wasn't comfortable with the hero tag, Kaleb had waltzed in here and saved her entire morning. And while looking after one's creature comforts might not seem very superheroesque, it meant everything to her. Not to mention, spoke volumes about the man behind it.

She started for her tent. Fortunately for her, she wasn't looking for a hero.

Kaleb stared at the computer screen, unable to contain the wide grin that spread across his face. A new tagline, new brochures and, now, a new website. Was there anything Grace couldn't do? In only a few days, she'd single-handedly changed the face of Mountain View Tours.

So, as the sun rose on a new week, it seemed only fitting they start revamping the front office, too. He'd picked up the paint from the hardware store this morning and his mom and sister, along with Grace's mother, were scheduled to be there at ten.

Excitement welled inside him. He could hardly wait for Memorial weekend and the grand opening of the *new* Mountain View Tours.

"Good morning." Grace breezed into the room, holding a can of Diet Dr Pepper, wearing torn, faded jeans, flip-flops and her leather jacket. Her long dark hair was pulled back in a ponytail and covered with a well-worn navy ball cap. Not her usual work attire, but then, he didn't make a habit of wearing holey cargos and a T-shirt left over from basic training either.

"Morning." He sipped his coffee. "And how was your Mother's Day?"

"It was quite nice actually." She paused at the counter. "After church, Roger took Mama and me out to dinner in Montrose and then we all went to the hot springs pool."

"That's weird. I saw Donna and Roger at church. How'd I miss you?"

"I…" Her gaze lowered momentarily before bouncing back to his. "Was taking advantage of my one and only day to sleep in."

Why did he get the feeling that Grace wasn't giving him the whole truth?

"What did you do yesterday?" Obviously eager to shift the conversation.

"Dad, Scott and I fixed dinner while Mom and Sami lost themselves in far too much HGTV."

"Where was Jack?"

"With us guys, of course."

"Ah, I see you got the paint." She eyed the three cans stacked against the wall.

"Yep. We're all set." He turned back to the computer. "Come here a minute. I need your opinion on something."

"Sure." She took a sip of her soda before joining him behind the counter. "What's up?"

"This." He pointed to the screen.

Setting her drink on the counter, she looked from the image back to him. "What am I looking at?"

"Carpet tiles." He reached for the mouse. "Let me show

you a better picture." He clicked on the image of a carpeted room.

She leaned in for a closer look. "Those are carpet tiles?"

"Yep."

"Wow. They look really nice." She straightened. "Are
they for your house?"

"No. They're for the office." He pointed to the un-
adorned floor.

"Really?" Her eyes were as big as her smile. "You mean
no more cold concrete?"

"That's right."

She perched a hand on her hip. "All right, who are you
and what have you done with Kaleb?"

"Very funny." He shifted his attention back to the computer screen, hoping she couldn't see the heat he felt creeping up his neck. "Let's just say I'm starting to see the
wisdom in what you and Sami have been saying."

"What was that?" She leaned closer. "I didn't quite hear
you." Grace was enjoying this way too much.

"You were right, okay. Are you happy now?"

Her satisfied grin said it all. "Ecstatic."

"I have to say—" he leaned against the low bookcase
behind the desk, crossing his arms over his chest "—I'm
pretty stoked about this makeover. Not to mention the grand
opening."

"Me, too." She shrugged out of her jacket, revealing a
paint-splattered United States Navy T-shirt. "I'm glad I
get to be part of it."

Moving to the opposite corner, she tossed her jacket onto
a limb of the coat tree. "Have you given any thought to this
counter?" Smoothing a hand along the finished wood top,
she made her way around to the other side. "We can work
with the top, maybe sand and restain it, but this particleboard on the front doesn't hold much potential."

"I thought you were planning to keep any more suggestions to yourself?" He followed her, liking the way she took such an interest in Mountain View Tours. As though it were important to her.

She lifted a shoulder. "I changed my mind." Still pondering the face of the reception desk, she said, "What if we covered it with some beadboard paneling, then painted it the same red as the trim."

"Hmm…" He rubbed his chin, trying to visualize the red.

The door opened then and a bearded man entered, carrying what appeared to be a file folder.

"Welcome to Mountain View Tours." Kaleb offered his hand.

The man took it. "Are you the owner?"

"Yes, sir. Kaleb Palmer."

"I'm Barry Swanson with the Bureau of Land Management." Since when did government agencies make personal visits?

Kaleb studied the man, who was slightly shorter than himself and wore wire-rimmed glasses. "What can I do for you, Mr. Swanson?"

"Barry, please." Still holding the folder, he crossed his hands in front of him. "As I'm sure you're aware, Jeep tour companies need permits from the BLM in order to operate on land owned by the forest service."

"Yes, I am aware of that."

"How long have you owned Mountain View Tours, Mr. Palmer?"

"Kaleb. Since the end of February." He assumed his at-ease stance, feet apart, hands clasped behind his back.

Barry opened the file folder. "I'm sorry, Kaleb, but we have no record of your request for permits."

"Mr. Chapman, the previous owner, said he had taken

care of them. That even though the business had changed owners, the permits would carry over."

Barry shook his head. "I'm afraid Mr. Chapman was mistaken. Not only did we not receive his paperwork, permits are not grandfathered in based on a change of ownership."

Kaleb's throat constricted. "I see. When is the paperwork due?"

Barry closed the file. "They were due in March."

Kaleb felt as if the air had been sucked out his lungs. All of his plans. The grand opening. He could almost hear the door slamming on his dreams.

Why hadn't he followed up on those permits and made sure they were taken care of? Instead, he was focused on trucks and Jeeps.

Panic wormed its way through his being. A feeling he knew well and despised.

"Mr. Swanson, I'm Grace McAllen, Mr. Palmer's office manager." She shook his hand. "I'm curious. Suppose Kaleb hadn't purchased the business until April or even this month. Would he still have been allowed to apply for the permits?"

"Yes, ma'am." The field officer tapped the file against his leg. "As I said, the permits do not carry over, so a new one would have to be issued, and then every subsequent year, the paperwork would be due in March."

Kaleb wasn't sure what Grace was up to, but she seemed to have a better mind for business than he did. So when she met his gaze, he issued a quick nod, urging her to continue.

Her attention returned to Mr. Swanson. "Since Kaleb was led to believe that the permits had not only been granted, but grandfathered in, is it possible you could extend him a little grace?"

The field officer appeared to mull over her request. He

studied Kaleb first, then the antiquated office. "Back when Dale Hannon owned this place, it ranked among the best tour companies in town."

Clearing his throat, Kaleb straightened, hands at his sides as though he were still in the army. "Yes, sir. And I intend to do everything in my power to show guests we're worthy of that distinction once again."

Lips pursed until his mouth disappeared behind his brownish-red beard, Barry nodded, still studying the space. Did he think it was a hopeless cause or was he recalling Mountain View Tours' former glory?

Finally, just when Kaleb thought he couldn't take it anymore, Barry opened the folder, pulled out a small stack of papers and handed them to Kaleb.

"You'll need to fill these out and provide all of the information listed there on the first page. Paperwork and fees will be due ASAP."

Relief washed over Kaleb, like air-conditioning on a steamy day.

"This is Monday…" said Grace. "What if we got them to you by, say, next Monday?"

Good plan. That would give them the weekend to work on things.

The man looked at Kaleb. "Do you have your general liability insurance?"

Kaleb nodded. "Yes, sir."

"Then let's shoot for Friday. Preferably by noon."

"This Friday?" For the first time, the despair Kaleb felt sparked in Grace's hazel eyes.

"Yes, ma'am."

What had they got themselves into? Neither he nor Grace knew anything about the paperwork Barry tasked them to do. And if there was one thing Kaleb knew about government agencies, it was that their paperwork was never easy.

He examined the documents in his hand, noting what all they required. "Any recommendations on how I come up with these estimates of land use?"

"Most people go back to their drivers' logs from previous years and base it off those numbers. Fees are based on the numbers you give. I know this is your first season, but you'll need to be as accurate as possible."

Accurate? How could they expect him to be accurate when he'd never done this before? And he didn't have a clue as to where the drivers' logs were, if there were even any here. Still…

"I understand," He shook the man's hand. "Thank you, sir."

As Mr. Swanson departed, Kaleb's gaze remained fixed on Grace. Not only had she gone to bat for him, as far as he was concerned, she'd hit a grand slam.

She shifted her weight from one foot to the other. Crossed her arms over her chest, looking everywhere but at him. "Okay, I know—I overstepped my boundaries and stuck my nose somewhere it didn't belong."

"You saved us, Grace." He raked a hand through his hair. "I was afraid he might shut us down on the spot. But you stepped up to the plate and saved Mountain View Tours. Thank you."

"You've worked hard, Kaleb. You don't deserve to have curveballs like that thrown at you." She cleared her throat. "So what do we have to do to get these permits?" She pointed to the papers.

He set them on top of the counter. "Let's see. Aside from a usage estimate, an operating plan, map of the areas we intend to access, copy of my current brochure…"

"Maps and brochures are easy enough. But the rest is going to take a while."

"No kidding. And we've only got four days." He drew in

a frustrated breath. "I sure hope we can find those drivers' logs. In the meantime, it looks like we'll have to postpone the painting."

"Postpone? Are you crazy?"

No, but she might have a screw loose. "Priorities, Grace. We have to start looking for the logs right away."

"We will. But you've got three people coming to paint. Let them paint while we work on the estimates. Because we will meet that deadline."

Chapter Seven

Grace ached for Kaleb. Why hadn't the forest service come to him sooner? Why did they wait until he was open for business?

It was what it was, though, and Grace was determined to see to it Kaleb met that deadline. Even if she wasn't quite sure how.

For two full days, they had been going through the previous owner's files, yet they'd located only about half of the drivers' logs. They'd searched the office and the shop. Drawers, cupboards, boxes. Kaleb had even gone so far as to call the former owner, who was confident all of the logs had been put into boxes and stowed in the shop.

Yet it was as if the other half had just disappeared. And from what Kaleb had told her about his former boss, they very well could have.

Still, they had to keep trying.

Kaleb was doing his best to remain positive, but failing miserably. The dark circles under his eyes told her he hadn't slept, and she had a feeling eating wasn't at the top of his priority list either. His frustration was almost palpable. And mounting with every hour that passed.

Paint fumes still hung in the air as Grace glanced from

the computer to the door that separated the office from the garage. She imagined Kaleb pacing through the shop, raking a hand through his hair as he scoured for more boxes, despite having gone through the place multiple times.

She jumped when Kaleb burst through the door and moved into the freshly painted office. His booted feet thudded against the concrete floor, the carpet tiles she was so looking forward to having been put on hold.

"I found another box. In the rafters, no less." Hoisting it onto the counter, he blew the dust off the top.

She hoped this one contained what they needed.

"Let's see what we've got." Behind the counter, Grace coughed, fanned the airborne particles with her hand and lifted the flaps. She pulled out a stack of papers and leafed through them.

Credit-card receipts from four years ago, followed by a wad of old rental agreements.

Peering inside the box, Kaleb grabbed another stack and sifted through them. "There doesn't seem to be any rhyme or reason to any of this." Bills marked with payment dates and check numbers, a to-go menu from some restaurant and gas receipts. "Ross was a worse businessman than I thought." He tossed the pile aside, the lines on his face growing more pronounced.

"But you're not." She rummaged through what was left inside the cardboard container. "You're conscientious and, unlike him, you care about your customers." She stopped her search, her spirits dipping another notch as she looked at Kaleb.

"No logs?"

She shook her head. "Sorry."

He shoved the box aside and started toward the shop. "I'm going to check the rafters again. See if I missed anything."

Moving around the counter, she stepped in front of him. "I think our time would be better spent if we stopped looking and started actually working on the estimates."

Hands on his hips, he glared down at her. "And how are we supposed to do that without the logs?"

"I don't know. But we're both smart people and you've been a guide for a long time. I'm sure we can figure something out."

Still staring at her, he pondered her suggestion. "I don't know." He scrubbed a hand over his face.

"Look, why don't we take a break? Maybe grab a bite to eat." Grace looked at the clock. "It's after one. I don't know about you, but I'm fading."

"I can't think about eating with this deadline hanging over my head. This is my life, Grace."

"I know it is. However, if you don't get some sustenance, you might not have a life to worry about." Moving back behind the counter, she grabbed her pack and unzipped it. "I think some food will revive us both. What are you in the mood for?" She pulled out her wallet. "Burgers or a sandwich?"

"You go on." He started toward the garage. "I've got to keep looking."

"And just how effective do you think you're going to be?"

He shot an annoyed glance over his shoulder.

Unwilling to be deterred, she again moved toward him. "You're exhausted, Kaleb. Both mentally and physically. You need food. Not to mention some fresh air to clear your head."

"I hired you to manage my office. Not me."

Instinct had her narrowing her eyes, though she quickly caught herself. "A good lunch will also improve your disposition. Now come on. We won't be gone that long."

Hunger audibly rumbled in his gut and she shot him a satisfied grin.

"All right." Changing directions, he aimed for the front door. "But just long enough to grab a quick bite."

Outside, she squinted against the midday sun, wishing she'd thought to grab her sunglasses. Temps were beyond perfect. Not too hot, not too cold. The kind of day no one wanted to be cooped up inside.

"So what'll it be?" Grace faced him, shielding her eyes with her hand.

"This way." He headed north at a pretty good clip. Despite his artificial leg, she practically had to double-step to keep up.

"What's the rush?"

Pausing, he whirled toward her, his fiery gaze boring into her. "Don't you get it? If I don't find those logs, I lose everything. Which means you'll be out of a job."

"That's not true and you know it." She wagged a finger in front of his face. "We can figure this out. But you need to chill."

With a growl, he started again, crossing Eighth Avenue at a brisk pace. "I'll relax once I get those permits."

"And how is Mountain View Tours' newest owner doing?" A cute strawberry blonde smiled up at Kaleb with a baby on her hip. "Whoa. You don't look so good, Kaleb."

"Thank you," Grace said behind him.

"Blakely, this is Grace, my office manager." He glanced her way. "Blakely owns Adventures in Pink over there on Seventh Avenue."

Ah, another Jeep tour place. "Blue building, right?"

"That's right." Blakely smiled, adjusting the adorable child, who was chewing on a set of toy keys. "It's nice to meet you."

Try as she might, Grace couldn't ignore the baby. "And who's this little cutie?"

"This is Katelynn." Blakely took hold of her daughter's arm and tried to make her wave. "Say 'Hi, Grace.'"

Katelynn was interested in only the keys.

Smoothing a hand across her daughter's back, Blakely again turned her attention to Kaleb. "So what's up? I've never seen you so downcast."

Grace looked from Blakely to Kaleb, suspecting Blakely more friend than foe. If that were the case, she might be able to advise Kaleb on how to come up with usage estimates. That was, if he were willing to ask.

"We're just busy gearing up for the season." He scratched a hand through his hair.

Perhaps Grace ought to stick her neck out and ask for him. Or at least prod him a bit. Of course, she might only succeed in irritating him even more. Though if it helped, it would definitely be worth it.

Grace held up a hand above her eyes to shield them from the sun. "How long have you been in the Jeep tour business, Blakely?"

Shifting the babe to her other hip, she said, "It was my grandfather's place, so practically all my life. This is my third year as owner, though."

"Wow. I bet you've got things down to a science, then. Like all the paperwork and things like permits?"

Blakely chuckled. "It took me a while, but I'm finally getting the hang of it. How are things going with you guys?"

Grace dared a glance at Kaleb. To her surprise, he actually appeared interested in the conversation. *Ask her, ask her...*

He drew in a deep breath.

Go on. Do it.

"You know the permits we have to get from the BLM?"

Grace mentally fist-pumped the air.

"Yes."

He hesitated a moment, seemingly surveying the mountains. "Any suggestions on how to come up with usage estimates?"

"I usually use the previous year's drivers' logs."

Kaleb looked at Blakely. "What if you didn't have them?"

"Oh." She thought for a moment. "Well, do you have any logs at all?"

"Less than half."

"Okay." Blakely nodded. "Did you happen to keep your own logs when you worked for Ross?"

"The last couple of years, yeah."

"So pull together everything you've got, your personal logs and whatever you have from the other drivers and come up with an average."

Grace couldn't help herself. "What a great idea."

"I guess that would work." Kaleb shrugged, but Grace could see the wheels turning.

Katelynn began to fuss.

Blakely stroked the child's dark hair. "Looks like somebody's ready for their nap." She faced Kaleb again. "I'd better run. But if you have any problems, please, don't hesitate to give me a call. I know how challenging it can be to get a grasp on some of this stuff."

"I will." He almost smiled as she walked away. "Thanks."

Arms crossed over her chest, Grace welcomed the breeze that skittered over her face as she stared up at her boss. "So, looks like there is another way to get those numbers."

Looking a little chagrined, he scraped his boot across the sidewalk. "I guess I should have listened to you."

"I want Mountain View Tours to succeed every bit as much as you do, you know."

"I fully believe that, Grace." He watched her with an

intensity she'd never seen before. "I apologize for giving you such a hard time."

Knowing she'd pushed the envelope enough for today, she lowered her arms. "Ah, don't worry about it. But I do have a question."

"What's that?"

"Do you know where *your* logs are?"

"Remember that room full of boxes?"

"Yeah." She cringed just thinking about it.

The corners of his mouth twitched. "There's a file cabinet tucked in the back. Everything is sorted by month and year."

This time she really did fist-pump the air. "Let's grab some lunch. Then we'll head to your house to get those files so we can start working on those estimates?"

"Sounds like a plan. But, Grace?" His smile evaporated.

"What?" She searched his gaze, fearful that she might have crossed another line by broaching the subject with Blakely.

He stared down at her, the light returning to his gray-green eyes. "Thank you for believing in me. And Mountain View Tours."

By the close of business Saturday, Kaleb was ready to celebrate. Not only had he and Grace met the designated BLM deadline yesterday, thanks to a temporary permit, they'd capped it off today with not only one, but two official tours.

Standing outside The Outlaw restaurant, Grace shot him a wary glance. "I thought we were going to work through some of your memorabilia tonight."

"We will. Right after we eat." That was, unless he could think of a way to get out of it. "But considering the week we've had, we deserve a little splurge."

"If you say so."

They moved past the clusters of people gathered outside and into the small, rustic restaurant that always bustled with activity.

Kaleb caught the eye of his friend Neil, the manager of The Outlaw, and held up two fingers.

After a quick perusal of the restaurant, Neil pointed to a corner table.

Kaleb waved his thanks.

As he and Grace moved toward their seats, he touched her elbow, urging her closer. "You like John Wayne?"

"I like steak more."

Did the woman know how to coerce a smile out of him or what? "Well, in case you're interested—" he pointed across the room "—there's his hat."

"Ooh..." Though her eyes were wide with feigned interest, she barely glanced at the well-worn cowboy hat on the wall.

Surrounded by the din of other patrons and ragtime music, they settled in at their table.

Grace picked up a menu, while Kaleb scanned the restaurant. He'd been here so many times he knew the menu by heart.

"I've always loved this place. Even as a kid."

Grace laid her menu down, her attention shifting to Kaleb. "What was it like growing up in Ouray?"

He shrugged, not giving it much thought. "Not so different from growing up anyplace else, I suppose. We just got into different kinds of trouble. And when we did, you could be certain that anyone who saw you not only knew who you were, but knew your parents, too." Resting his forearms on the table, he leaned forward. "I remember this one time—I guess I was about seven—my friend Max and I were trying to climb the rocks at Cascade Falls—"

"That's near town, right? I've seen the sign."

He blinked. "Wait a minute. You've been here for almost two weeks and you haven't been to Cascade Falls? How is that even possible? I mean, for most people, it's one of their first stops."

Looking a tad sheepish, she leaned back in her chair. "I'm working all the time."

He sent her a perturbed look. "No, you're not."

Apparently out of excuses, she remained silent.

"Okay, we need to hurry up and order. Because we're going to Cascade Falls."

"Tonight?"

"Yes."

An hour later, after Grace had tackled every last scrap of her New York strip like a Broncos linebacker, they exited the restaurant into the mild evening air.

Main Street was alive with shoppers, onlookers and those happily enjoying ice cream on one of the town's many benches as they took in the scenery. He and Grace headed north, dodging young and old alike, as well as the occasional four-legged canine friend. Though Memorial Day weekend was still a week away, the town's population had already begun to swell. Only a precursor of what was to come as they headed into the high season.

With Grace at his side, they turned onto Eighth Avenue and continued east, the rocky road growing steeper with every step. Behind them, the sun slid below the mountains and, while it was still daylight, shadows had begun to fall over Ouray.

"Perhaps we should do this another time. Earlier in the day." Grace sounded a bit winded. "I mean, what about the stuff for the museum?"

"Sorry, Grace, but I cannot let another day pass without you experiencing Cascade Falls."

"Why?" She stopped.

So did he. "Because it's very important to me."

She let go a sigh. "Lead on, then."

Before long, the sound of rushing water touched their ears.

"Are we getting close?" Her expression was hopeful.

"Yep. Keep walking."

"Just so you'll know—" she huffed and puffed "—my muscles are burning. Doesn't this climb bother your leg?"

"Nah. I'm used to it." He slowed his pace so she could catch up. "This was my first stop after returning home." He loved this place. Always had. But even more so since the IED.

Excitement coursed through him as the falls came into view. He couldn't wait to see Grace's reaction. Stepping out of the way, he glimpsed the slow smile that overtook her face.

"Oh, Kaleb."

The sight of silvery-white water as it plummeted over some ten stories of craggy rocks never ceased to move him. And the roar of the falls, coupled with the gentle breeze that carried the songs of sparrows, filled him with a peace he longed to share with Grace. Because for all of her business smarts, all her plans, something was amiss. At times, he'd detect a deep sadness, an emptiness. If only he could find out what it was.

"Let's get closer." He nudged her across the wooden bridge and onto a narrow path. When they emerged, they were on the other side of the stream, mere feet from the falls.

The gentle mist touched their skin.

Grace rubbed her arms. "This is…stunning." Closing her eyes, she inhaled deeply. When she opened them, she peered up at him through thick lashes. "Thank you for urging me to come up here."

As daylight faded into night, he looked down at her. "You can't simply be in Ouray, Grace. You've got to experience it." Whether it was the faith she had in him or her genuine desire to make Mountain View Tours a success, Grace stirred something in him that had been long dormant. Something he'd do well to ignore since she'd be leaving at the end of the summer.

"You said this was the first place you came after coming home. Why is it so special to you?"

Taking a step back, he shoved his hands in the pockets of his jeans and took in the familiar surroundings. "It never changes." He had to raise his voice to be heard over the falls. "Sure it might appear different throughout the seasons, and nature sometimes has a way of relandscaping—" he gestured to the boulders and logs that littered the valley floor "—but the falls, the mountain… They're unchanging." He turned toward her now. "They remind me that while that IED may have changed my body, the God that lives inside me never changes. And regardless of what I've lost, He's promised me so much more."

With the slightest tilt of her head, she watched him, her gaze probing. "You really believe that, don't you?"

"With all my heart. The way I see it, when the going gets tough, we can either cling to God or run away." He shook his head. "But it's impossible to outrun God."

Her brow lifted. "I think your faith may have faltered a bit this week. When you were freaking out over the drivers' logs."

Chagrined, he lowered his head. God had brought him through far worse, and yet, instead of reflecting on God's faithfulness, Kaleb worried. *Forgive my unbelief, Lord.*

His gaze met Grace's. "You're right. Instead of trusting

in God to provide, I trusted in myself. And I failed. I'm just glad God didn't."

Nodding, she toed a rock. "I'm curious, then. What was your reaction when you found out you'd lost your leg?"

The evening air stirred then, sending a shiver up his spine.

"Mind if we sit down?" He gestured toward a massive boulder that sat several feet away.

As daylight faded, they eased onto the rock, close enough that they wouldn't have to yell to hear each other over the rushing water.

Grace wrapped her arms around herself.

"Are you cold?"

"Cool, but I'll be okay."

He drew in a deep breath. "To answer your question, when I first heard about my leg, I wished I'd died with my buddies." He saw Grace's body sag. "For six months, I merely existed in that hospital, doing whatever they told me to do. But deep inside—" he pointed to his chest "—I'd given up. I'd lost my leg, my fiancée and, as far as I was concerned, my life."

She straightened. "You were engaged?"

"Her name was Gina. She was tough as nails. Or so I thought. But as soon as the going got tough, she bailed. I'm just thankful I discovered that little character flaw before we said 'I do.'"

Grace's gaze drifted to the turbulent stream in the distance. "Sometimes people profess to love without ever really knowing what it truly means."

The remark caught him off guard. Somehow, he didn't think she was talking about Gina.

Looking at him again, she said, "What brought you back around?"

"Sami."

Grace's eyes widened. "Really? What did she do?"

"She showed me a picture."

"Of what?"

"Jack. Of course, we didn't know it was Jack yet."

Grace appeared confused.

"It was Jack's first sonogram. Kind of looked like a gerbil to me—"

Her soft chuckle eased the inevitable, albeit momentary, grief that usually accompanied his story.

"While I pretended not to listen, Sami went on about how she'd always looked up to me and how she wanted her baby to do the same. She told me to stop feeling sorry for myself. To stop focusing on what I'd lost and thank God for everything I still had. Then she taped that picture where I'd be sure to see it."

"What did you do?"

"Continued to sulk. But the more I looked at that picture, something grabbed hold of my heart. Not only did I want to meet my niece or nephew, I wanted to be part of his or her life. To teach them all those things Sami and I used to do when we were kids. Suddenly, Jack became my reason to live."

"That explains why you're so close to him now."

"Yeah. I couldn't love that kid any more if he were my own."

"He's lucky to have you."

"I don't know about that. I tend to look at it the other way around."

Hands clasped in her lap, Grace studied them for a moment. "I can't imagine how difficult it was to learn about your buddies."

He stared at the falls, nodded, his throat too thick to respond.

"But I don't understand why you don't want to see their

families. I mean, you were the last one to see their loved ones alive. You're their last connection."

The words slammed into his chest, burrowing their way into that dark part of him he refused to let anybody see. Yet somehow it rose to the surface.

"I'm the reason my friends are dead." He cringed the moment the words left his mouth.

"Wha—"

He stood, refusing to discuss it anymore. "It's dark. I'll walk you home."

Chapter Eight

The aroma of fresh-popped popcorn filled the air in front of Mountain View Tours on Memorial Day. Inside, the front office had been completely transformed. From the carpet tiles to the freshly painted walls, everything had been revived.

Finally, with all of the obstacles behind him, Kaleb could relax and enjoy the grand-opening festivities. He felt as though this entire weekend had been one big party. The weather was perfect, every tour was full and the number of people sharing in the fun was beyond anything he'd imagined.

God had knocked this one out of the ballpark.

And to think, Grace almost kept the idea to herself. Boy, was he glad Sami had coaxed it out of her. This weekend had been exactly the kind of kickoff he'd dreamed about, yet had no clue how to execute. Thanks to Grace, though, that dream was now a reality and the *new* Mountain View Tours was on its way to reclaiming its once-glowing reputation. Something that was bound to bring in more business.

Wearing a pair of denim capris and a sleeveless white blouse, Grace filled another batch of red-white-and-blue helium balloons at the table just outside the entrance.

Times like this, he wondered where he'd be without her. Despite a somewhat rocky start, she had quickly exceeded his expectations for an office manager. And so much more.

Grace seemed to know him inside and out. At times she'd push hard, though she also knew when to back off. Like last weekend, when he'd blurted out something that was better left unsaid. She hadn't brought it up since.

A patriotic song echoed from the docking station behind Grace, sending Kaleb's gaze to the four American flags swaying in the breeze along the front of the building. One for each of the four men who were with him that day in Afghanistan.

His gut churned as regret and sorrow flooded his inner being. If only he'd seen that trip wire. Swallowing around the sudden lump in his throat, he tilted his face heavenward. *God, I don't know why You chose to spare me, but I pledge myself to You once again and ask that You would use me in whatever manner You see fit.*

He took a deep breath. *Thank You, God, for the privilege of knowing each of those men and I ask a special blessing upon their families.*

Their families. In just a little under a month those families would be coming to Ouray, expecting to see him and spend time with him and, no doubt, wanting to talk about their loved ones. Grace was right. He was their last connection. Wives and parents were probably curious about their last days.

Early on, after he settled back in Ouray, he'd spoken to a couple of them on the phone. But that was different. He didn't have to look them in the eye.

Returning his focus to the flags, he knew that Memorial Day would never be the same for him. He'd fought alongside men who gave their lives for this country. They were his friends and he would not let them be forgotten.

A tapping against his thigh had him looking down. Jack stared up at him through his star-shaped sunglasses. The innocence on his nephew's face chased away Kaleb's morose.

"What's up, Jack?" He lifted the child into his arms.

"I wanna dwive."

The kid loved it when Kaleb let him play in the trucks. "You want to drive, huh?"

Jack nodded emphatically.

"We need to see what your folks have to say about that one, buddy." Kaleb strode toward the table where Sami and her husband, Scott, were tying long ribbons on the freshly inflated balloons.

"Somebody wants to do some driving." He nodded to the bright blue rental Jeep he had on display in front of the building. Not only was it for people to have a look-see, they'd had kids hopping in and out all weekend for photo ops. "Told him we'd have to check with you."

"Sure. But, Jack—" Sami sent her son that motherly warning look "—I want you to sit on your bottom. No standing, you hear me?"

"Yes, ma'am." Jack turned his attention to Grace. "Wanna wide wif me, Gwace?" The kid had really taken a liking to her.

Kaleb couldn't say that he blamed him. He'd kind of taken a liking to her, too.

"I'd love to, Jack, but I need to help your uncle Kaleb. Can I take a rain check?"

Jack's expression turned serious. "It's not waining, Gwace."

She smiled. "You're right. It's not. Silly me."

"Maybe Grace can ride with you later." Kaleb moved toward the vehicle, opened the door and deposited Jack in the driver's seat. He moved the seat as far forward as it would go. "What's the first thing we do when we get into a vehicle?"

"Seat belt!"

"That's right." Kaleb grabbed the restraint and reached across his nephew to secure it. "You're ready to roll, soldier."

"Close the doow."

He pushed the door closed, taking a moment to listen to the vrooming noises coming from Jack. Chuckling to himself, he turned to rejoin the other adults.

An older couple stood at the table, looking over a brochure as Grace spoke with them.

"Yes, we do still have some openings on our tours for tomorrow. Were you looking at morning or afternoon?" She eyed him as he approached. "Kaleb, this is Mr. and Mrs. Russell." Her focus returned to the couple. "Kaleb is the owner of Mountain View Tours."

"Good to meet you, son." Mr. Russell held out his hand.

Kaleb accepted, noticing the Desert Storm Veteran insignia on the man's ball cap. "What branch of the military were you in?"

"Army. Second Armored Division."

Kaleb smiled. "Hundred and First Airborne Division. Operation Enduring Freedom."

"A man who knows what Memorial Day is truly about." Mr. Russell gestured to the decorations.

"Yes, sir." Far better than he cared to.

Someone screamed and Kaleb instinctively scanned the area, his heart leaping into his throat.

Jack!

The Jeep was rolling down Mountain View Tours' drive, aimed for the street. Sweat beaded his forehead as he rushed toward it.

People scrambled to get out of the way. One man attempted to reach the passenger door, but missed.

With a final lunge, Kaleb grabbed hold of the driver's door and flung it open. His pulse and the Jeep were the only things that seemed to be moving quickly. People had moved into the street, waving their arms to stop oncoming traffic.

Holding tight to the door, Kaleb lifted himself enough to get his right foot inside and on the brake pedal. The Jeep jerked to a stop.

Glancing at the line of cars now stopped in the northbound lane, he breathed a sigh of relief.

Then the applause started. Just a couple of people at first, and then more joined in until it thundered around him.

"That was fun." Jack cheered.

Kaleb released the buckle. "Scoot over, Jack." His nephew climbed over the center console and Kaleb hopped in. And that was when he saw it.

The emergency brake wasn't set. And the gearshift was in Neutral.

He could have killed Jack. Why hadn't he double-checked the brake when he put Jack in the Jeep?

He quickly returned the vehicle to its original position, regret beating like a woodpecker against his rib cage. Once again, he'd allowed himself to become distracted, risking the lives of those around him.

Sami snagged her son from the passenger side, pressing his little body against hers as she held him close. "Oh, thank God, you're okay, baby." She kissed his face, but Jack was oblivious to all the commotion.

"I was dwiving, Mama."

"You sure were, son." Scott reached for the boy. "But that's enough for one day."

Sami met Kaleb as he stepped out of the Jeep. "Once a hero, always a hero." Slipping her arms around him, she fell against him in a powerful hug. "Thank you, big brother."

He was no hero. Not now, not ever.

He grabbed his sister by the arms, breaking her hold, and stepped back. "The parking brake was off."

Her liquid eyes searched his.

Raking a disgusted hand through his hair, he tried unsuccessfully to quell the storm raging inside him. "It was my fault that the Jeep rolled into the street."

Sami shook her head. "But you saved him."

He glared at her now. "It shouldn't have happened in the first place." Walking past his sister, he ignored the crowd that had gathered and continued into the deepest corner of the garage. The smell of petroleum and rubber hung heavy in the air.

Tilting his head up, he blinked away the tears that blurred his vision. *God, thank You for protecting Jack. Forgive me for not paying closer attention.*

So much for restoring the company's reputation.

"You okay?" He should have known Grace would follow him.

He turned away, not wanting her to see him like this. "Yeah."

"I heard what you said to Sami."

Great. Now she knew just how incompetent he was.

"You're wrong, though."

He sensed her moving closer.

"Danny was the one who parked that Jeep. If anyone—"

Unwilling to listen to any of her excuses, he whirled to face her. "I'm the owner. I should have checked the parking brake."

"It was an accident, Kaleb. No one *meant* for it to happen."

"It did happen, though."

"And you saved the day. Jack is safe because of you. In my book, that's a hero."

He blew out a disbelieving laugh. "Heroes don't allow things to happen in the first place."

"No, because no one can control everything."

Touché.

Locked in a staredown with his office manager, he drew in a deep breath, willing his pulse to a normal rate. "In here—" he pointed to his head "—I know you're right. But my heart has a hard time accepting that what happened to my buddies, what happened to Jack, wasn't my fault. If I'd have done just one thing differently, like check the parking brake, or not allowed myself to become distracted, I could have changed the outcome."

Taking a step closer, Grace laid a hand on his forearm, sending a wave of awareness through him. "Kaleb, we all second-guess ourselves." She cocked her head, making her appear more thoughtful. "Do you believe in God's providence? That He has a plan and a purpose for everything?"

"Yes."

"Then why are you trying to put yourself above God by second-guessing what He allowed to happen?"

Was that what he'd been doing?

He stood there, paralyzed, as conviction rained down on him. "Is that what you think I've been doing?"

Grace didn't say a word, simply lifted a brow as if to say, "What do you think?"

My ways are not your ways.

"I think you've just opened my eyes, Grace." He laid his hand atop hers. "Thank you for the perspective."

"You're welcome." She pulled her hand away then.

"I didn't realize you'd spent so much time in God's word."

"I did a lot of Bible studies while I was deployed." Rubbing her arms, she took a step back.

"That's great." He stepped toward her, thrilled with the knowledge that Grace was a woman of faith. "I know I need my daily dose of the Bible every morning. Maybe we—"

"I'd better get back outside."

Grace had fallen in love with Ouray. The beauty, the history, the sense of community… Though there were days when she wished she were aboard that cruise ship, away from the lure of what-ifs and what-could-have-beens.

This was one of those days.

Still frustrated over her conversation with Kaleb yesterday, she unlocked the post office box and peered inside. She welcomed the opportunity, no matter how small it might be, to get out of the office and enjoy a little fresh air, away from her increasingly handsome boss.

Oftentimes, when she was at sea, she'd sneak away from the engine room and make her way topside to fill her lungs with something besides jet fuel vapors and soak up a little vitamin D.

It was also where she would talk to God, keeping Him as her anchor when she was half a world away from those she loved.

A lot of good that did her.

Unlike Kaleb, she wasn't second-guessing what God allowed to happen.

God had failed her. He took her dad, made her unable to conceive and then allowed her husband to fall into the arms of another woman who was able to give him a child. Grace was better off on her own, not trusting in a God who seemed eager to knock her down at every turn.

So who was she to go spouting off spiritual truths? Leading Kaleb to believe she was some faith-filled woman when her faith had died right along with her dreams of a family.

Shaking off the depressing thoughts, she retrieved the short stack of mail and locked the box before making her way back through the glass double doors onto Main Street.

Kaleb was the kind of man Grace had once dreamed of finding. A man who did his best to live out his faith in word and deed. A man who would never be interested in a woman whose faith was on the skids. And yet her sleep was plagued with dreams of him.

The subconscious mind could be so annoying.

Strolling down the sidewalk, she paused in front of one of the gift shops to study their window display. She'd been wanting to pick up a T-shirt or two, but was having a hard time deciding which ones she liked best.

Unfortunately, she didn't dare waste too much time. Over the past few days, business at Mountain View Tours had shifted into high gear. This morning alone, they'd had six tours, half a dozen phone inquiries and at least twice that many from the website. And the season had barely begun. At this rate, she'd never keep up.

Kaleb was beyond ecstatic and she was happy for him. He'd worked hard, putting his heart and soul into this business, and deserved to be rewarded.

Still undecided about the T-shirts, she gave up and proceeded on to the deli to pick up a couple of sandwiches for her and Kaleb.

Lunch in hand, she made her way back to the office, pausing to admire one of the gorgeous flower baskets that hung from every lamppost along Main Street. Ouray was the kind of charming little town she used to envision calling home. The picture of Americana, complete with white picket fences, colorful old buildings and purple mountains' majesty. A place that made her want to put down roots.

She blew out a frustrated breath and moved on, approaching Mountain View Tours as one of their morning tours returned. Kaleb was outside, greeting everyone and asking if they'd enjoyed their tour. As if he couldn't tell from the smiles on their faces. Perhaps once they heard the news that Corkscrew and Engineer Pass had opened ahead of schedule, they'd be ready to sign up for another outing tomorrow.

Which meant she'd better get inside.

Her cell phone rang. With the bag containing their lunch dangling from her left hand, she tucked the mail under the same arm and retrieved the phone from her back pocket.

One glance at the screen sent her heart into a tailspin.

Why would Aaron be calling her?

A hundred scenarios clamored through her brain, none of them making any sense. Once upon a time, she'd prayed that he would call, telling her he'd made a mistake and begging her to take him back. That call never came. And even if this was it, she'd tell him in no uncertain terms that she had no interest in reconciliation. Something she couldn't have said a year ago.

The phone continued to ring, her angst building with each jingle. She could simply let it go to voice mail and see if he left a message. But if he didn't, she'd be left wondering why he called.

With a shaky breath, she touched the accept icon and put the phone to her ear.

"Hello."

"Grace. Hey, it's Aaron." As if she didn't already know that.

Keep it light. Upbeat. "Hey, Aaron. How's it going?" Ugh. Nothing like trying too hard.

"Pretty good. Just busy. AJ is crawling now." He chuckled. "The kid's into everything."

As if she wanted to hear that tidbit of information.

"But, hey, that's not why I'm calling."

No "How are you?" or "How's it going?" In typical Aaron fashion, he forged right ahead with his agenda, never even bothering to ask where she was or what she'd been up to.

"Tessa and I have found a house we want to buy."

Funny, last time Grace checked, he had a house. A house he'd once shared with her.

"Which is why I'm calling. In your rush to leave Jacksonville, you failed to sign the quitclaim deed."

Rush to leave? He'd turned her world upside down. Left her for another woman, one who happened to be carrying his child. Something Grace wasn't able to give him. Aaron had practically deemed her worthless, in front of God and everybody. Why on earth would she want to hang around any longer than she had to?

Dropping onto a nearby bench, she allowed her gaze to roam the mountaintops, finding the strength to temper her flailing emotions. "What's a quitclaim deed?"

"A form that basically states you no longer have an interest in the house and removes your name from the deed, freeing me up to sell it."

No interest? The house where she'd spent countless hours stripping wallpaper, painting and tearing out flooring. Where she'd learned to tile bathrooms and backsplashes and lay hardwood floors. All in an effort to call it her own. The house that was supposed to be her haven. A place she could finally call home. Where she'd settle down and raise a family.

How could she possibly have no interest? Even though he did pay her half of what little equity they had in the house.

"We need to move quickly on this other house, Grace. So would it be all right if I overnighted you the form?"

The final piece of her once-seemingly-happy life was being ripped from her already-bloodied hands. Just like every other dream she'd had.

A tempestuous storm arose in her gut, churning with fury. How could she have loved someone so heartless?

Perhaps she should refuse to sign the form. Tell him she wasn't interested in selling.

But that was Aaron's style, not hers.

Her body sagging, she dropped her head in her hand and stared at the sidewalk. "Yeah. Send it on."

"Awesome. I just need your address."

Knowing she'd be at work, she gave the address for Mountain View Tours.

"Thanks, Grace."

Ending the call, she glared at the screen, feeling as though she might be sick.

"Everything all right?"

She jerked her head up to find Kaleb standing over her.

"Yeah." She forced herself to smile and pushed to her feet. "Why wouldn't it be?"

"I don't know." Kaleb's gray-green gaze narrowed. "But whoever you were talking to, you didn't look too happy."

"Oh, that." She returned the phone to her back pocket, determined not to let Kaleb see what a mess she was inside. "It was nothing."

Arms crossed over his chest, he continued to scrutinize her. "You know—" his deeper-than-usual voice didn't bode well "—over these past few weeks you've gotten to know me pretty well. You've pushed and prodded, getting me to tell you things I've never told anyone else. But there's not a whole lot I know about you."

Which was how she preferred it. Because if she let someone like Kaleb in, her heart might never survive.

"Sure there is." Looking everywhere but at him, she adjusted the bag on her arm. "I hope you're hungry. I picked up your favorite sandwich from the deli. Not to mention some of those homemade kettle chips."

"Grace…"

She hated it when he said her name like that. So comforting and inviting. Yet edged with warning.

Quickly herding her scattered emotions, she forced herself to look him in the eye. "Yes?"

His smile was slow as his arms fell to his sides. Shaking his head, he took the bag from her hand. "Let's go eat."

She followed him into the office, breathing a sigh of relief. As wound up as she was, if Kaleb had pressed her, she might have lost it right there on Main Street. And that was so not her.

However, with Aaron's request hanging over her head, her nerves would remain as frayed as that worn-out pair of jeans she kept in the bottom of her footlocker. If Kaleb decided to push her the way she'd pushed him…

She couldn't let that happen. Wouldn't let that happen. Because she'd never let anyone past her defenses again.

Chapter Nine

Kaleb wanted nothing more than to help Grace. As was typical of his office manager, though, she tried to act as though all was well. But from the moment he saw her sitting on that bench yesterday, he knew she was hurting. The pain in her eyes when she looked up at him only confirmed his suspicions.

Now, standing at the top of Engineer Pass, hands jammed in the pockets of his jeans, he looked out over the surrounding peaks. Despite a mild winter and an early spring, patches of grass still battled snow for ownership of the gray, barren rock below, while pale gray clouds blanketed much of the sky.

He wished Grace would have come. Perhaps the change of scenery would have taken her mind off whatever troubled her. Yet even though Sami had offered to fill in, Grace had declined his invitation, claiming she had too much paperwork to do.

Turning, he watched his guests as they took pictures atop the rocky peak, hoping to capture the beauty around them. Memories they'd carry home to share with family and friends.

He was in his element, doing what he loved. Helping

others experience things they otherwise might never see. Memories in the making.

So why did he feel so lousy?

Grace.

In the few weeks that he'd known her, she'd challenged him in ways no one ever had. She pushed him to look within himself and find the strength to overcome the torment he still harbored inside. And while he had a long way to go, he wished he could do the same for her.

"Excuse me, Kaleb?" He turned to see two of his guests—Mr. and Mrs. Higgins, as he recalled—a couple close to his parents' age.

Mrs. Higgins held out a camera. "Would you mind taking our picture?"

He couldn't help smiling. "That's what I'm here for."

The couple wrapped their arms around each other, fitting together as if each were designed specifically for the other.

"We're celebrating our thirtieth wedding anniversary," said Mr. Higgins.

"Congratulations." Kaleb aimed the camera. "Let's make this a good one, then."

The couple's smiles were filled with joy, their love evident by the glint in their eyes.

Kaleb took two shots for good measure, then handed the camera back, a sudden loneliness leaching into his heart.

He longed to find that kind of love. That one person God created just for him. Who loved him despite his flaws and that he couldn't imagine living without.

Shaking away the thought, he addressed the seven people he'd had the pleasure of taking on a tour today. "Okay, folks. Time to wrap things up."

A few rushed to take some last-minute photos, while others climbed back onto the tour truck.

Once everyone was loaded and accounted for, Kaleb began their descent down the mountain. Sharp, jagged rocks littered the road, meaning he had to move at a snail's pace or risk jostling his guests right out of the vehicle. They didn't seem to mind, though. Instead, they were mesmerized by the fourteen-foot snowbanks that lined both sides of the narrow road.

When they arrived back in Ouray a couple of hours later, Kaleb assisted his guests as they exited the truck, taking the time to thank each of them for choosing Mountain View Tours. Without them, there wouldn't be a Mountain View Tours.

"We were thinking about renting one of your Jeeps for tomorrow," said Mr. Higgins. "Do you think that would be possible?"

Beside him, his wife clung to his arm, anticipation evident in her eager smile.

"Absolutely. And it would give you two the opportunity to do some exploring on your own."

The man glanced at his wife. "That's what we were thinking."

"Well, if you'd like to come inside, we'll get you all set up."

They followed him through the front door.

"Grace, Mr. and Mrs. Higgins would like to rent a Jeep."

Behind the desk, she jerked her head up, her smile a little too forced, failing to reach her eyes. "Sure." She hopped off the stool and grabbed a clipboard with the paperwork. "I'll just need you to fill these out."

"Grace will get you squared away. If you have any questions or problems, though, don't hesitate to let me know."

"Great. Thank you, Kaleb." The man waved as Kaleb headed back outside.

After removing the cooler and blankets from the truck,

along with any trash, he pulled out the hose and sprayed the vehicle down, his thoughts repeatedly drifting to Grace. Something troubled her. Was she unhappy in Ouray? Was there a problem with her mother or Roger?

The cell phone attached to the clip on his belt vibrated.

Releasing the sprayer to stop the flow of water, he retrieved the phone and looked at the screen.

Vanessa.

His body tensed. Why was she calling him now? Had something happened? Had they decided not to come to Ouray after all?

Wishful thinking.

Dropping the hose, he pressed the accept icon. "Hey, Vanessa. How's it going?" The words came out with far more enthusiasm than he felt.

"Wonderful."

He scratched a hand through his hair. "How's Hannah?"

"She's good. And very much looking forward to our trip to Ouray."

"Glad to hear it." He often worried about Beau's little girl. Growing up without a dad was never easy.

"How's that new business of yours?"

"Great." He eyed the steady stream of vehicles easing their way up Main Street, grateful for the small talk. "We had our grand opening this weekend."

"Congratulations. I know how much this means to you, Kaleb. Beau used to share your stories about Jeeping and the mountains and say that we had to make plans to go to Ouray one day."

Kaleb's chest constricted. What he wouldn't give to make that happen.

"That reminds me. I was looking around the Ouray website the other day and saw that there's going to be some ribbon-cutting ceremony while we're there and that you're one of the guests."

He cleared his throat. "At the museum. Yes."

"That's fantastic. Why didn't you tell us?"

The knot in his stomach twisted. He shouldn't have agreed to speak. Especially not when he knew his friends' families were going to be here.

"Sorry, guess it slipped my mind. You know, with business and all."

"I understand."

He breathed a sigh of relief.

"Okay, so I just wanted to go over a few details, make sure we're all on the same page." Vanessa rattled off arrival dates, who all was coming and where they'd be staying.

"Sounds good." He watched an express delivery truck as it pulled alongside the curb. "We'll see you on June twenty-first, then."

"And, Kaleb?"

"Yes?"

"You will take us on one of your tours, right?"

For Beau's sake—"Absolutely."

While Kaleb clipped the phone back on his belt, the driver of the delivery truck emerged, carrying a large envelope. Spotting Kaleb, his pace quickened. "I've got a delivery for a—" he eyed the address label "—Grace McAllen."

Who would be sending Grace an express package?

Curiosity got the best of him, so rather than directing the driver inside, Kaleb said, "I'll make sure she gets it."

"Just sign here." The driver held out his device and Kaleb jotted his signature on the screen. "Thanks. Have a good one."

Kaleb allowed his gaze to fall to the return address. *Aaron McAllen. Jacksonville, Florida.*

A brother, perhaps?

Hmm… He'd heard mention of a sister, but no brother.

He knew Jacksonville had been her last assignment, but not necessarily her home.

Unless… His heart sank.

Grace was married.

But wouldn't she have said something? Or worn a ring?

A car horn jolted him back to reality.

Grace's marital status was none of his business.

He lowered the envelope and started toward the office, wishing he'd directed the driver inside after all. Maybe then he wouldn't have this sudden ache in his chest.

He pushed open the door, noting that she was alone. "Grace."

She looked across the desk, strands of her long hair escaping the clip that was supposed to be holding it up. "Yes."

"A package came for you." He approached, laying the envelope on the counter.

She glanced at it, then at him, just long enough for him to glimpse the sorrow swimming in her eyes.

"You okay?"

With a quick shake of her head, she grabbed the package and turned away. "Yeah. Everything's great." Definite overkill on the cheerfulness. Meaning things weren't as great as she claimed.

He didn't like to see her hurting and found himself wishing he could take her into his arms and make whatever was troubling her go away. But he knew Grace well enough to know that she'd only push him away. She wasn't the type to share her burdens. No matter how much she might want to.

If only he could make her understand that she could trust him. That he was here for her and wanted to be her friend.

For whatever reason, though, trust didn't come easy

to Grace. Now he could only wonder if Aaron McAllen wasn't part of the reason why.

Grace locked the front door of Mountain View Tours and flipped the sign from Open to Closed, feeling like a can of soda that had been tossed around and was ready to spew. Aaron's phone call had hung over her like a dark cloud all last night and into today.

Now the final piece of her shattered dreams had arrived in the form of a quitclaim deed, with a note that read "Thanks, Grace. You're the best."

Obviously she wasn't the best or Aaron wouldn't have betrayed her in the first place.

She needed to get out of here, find someplace to vent. Someplace safe where she could rant about her troubles and no one would know. Perhaps a long ride on her motorcycle.

She grabbed her pack from beneath the counter, tucked the express envelope inside then went into the garage to let Kaleb know she was leaving.

Amid the smells of various petroleum products, he stood at the long workbench, sorting through tools and putting them away.

She slipped her pack over her shoulder. "I'm heading out."

He turned, his easy smile replaced by a look of concern. "I know I already asked you, but are you sure you're all right, Grace?"

No getting anything past Mr. Perceptive. Yet for as much as she longed to pour her heart out to him, she didn't trust herself. He was the kind of guy who would listen attentively and do his best to comfort her. And the comforting was what worried her. It would be so easy to fall into his strong arms and believe that all was right with the world.

So, for her boss's sake as much as her own, she'd just have to fake it. "Yeah. I'm just a little tired, that's all."

"I hope you're not getting sick." He moved toward her, his concern mounting.

"I'm fine. I just…" *Tell him. Give the guy a chance.* "I didn't sleep well last night." No fibbing there.

Wiping his hands on a shop rag, he continued to study her. "That would explain the bags under your eyes."

Did he just— "Bags? What do you mean—"

He laughed. "There's the spitfire we all know and love."

Love?

Still laughing, he lowered his arms, closed the distance between them and gave her a hug. "Sleep well, Grace." He smelled of fresh air and masculinity. A toxic mix for someone in her pathetic state. And she missed him as soon as he stepped away. "And remember, I'm always here if you need me." The sincerity in those gray-green depths nearly had her spilling everything right there in the garage.

Yet, somehow, she managed to hold herself together. "I appreciate that. But I'll be fine."

Outside, she waited at the corner for traffic to clear, wishing for the millionth time that her father was still alive. He'd know exactly what to say to make her feel better.

Hands shoved in her pockets, she crossed the street, continuing aimlessly onto the sidewalk. After all this time, after what he did, Aaron still expected her to jump through hoops for him. The gall of that—

"Grace?"

She looked up to see her mother standing in front of the hardware store, holding a plastic bag in each hand, worry lines creasing her brow.

"Mama." A morsel of peace that hadn't been there a moment ago settled in Grace's heart.

"What's wrong, baby?"

Tears sprang to Grace's eyes and she had to work double time to blink them away.

Shifting both bags to one hand, Mama wrapped her free arm around Grace. "Come on. Let's go back to the house so we can talk."

Grace simply nodded, knowing that if she tried to speak, the tears she was desperately trying to fend off would overtake her right there. And that was a sight nobody wanted to see. Especially her.

By the time they arrived at Mama and Roger's house, Grace had regained her composure. Now in the living room of the quiet two-story, she and her mother sat on the white-slipcovered sofa, shoes off, legs tucked under them as they faced each other.

"Where's Roger?"

"Bowling at the Elks Lodge."

"There's a bowling alley at the Elks Lodge?" The historic brick building didn't look that big.

"A two-lane bowling alley."

"Two lanes?"

Mama nodded. "The whole setup is an antique. We'll have to take you over there sometime." She reached for Grace's hand. "Now tell me, what's got you so down?"

Grace drew in a shaky breath. "I didn't think it possible for Aaron to hurt me any more than he already has." She shrugged as tears again sprang to her eyes. "But I guess I was wrong."

"Oh, baby." Mama scooted closer and wrapped Grace in her arms. "I'm so sorry."

Whether unable or unwilling to resist, Grace melted against her mother, her tears falling freely, perhaps for the first time, as she grieved for everything she'd lost. Clinging to Mama, Grace poured out every hurt, every disappointment.

All the while, Mama held her close, stroking her hair, her back. A comforting touch Grace hadn't felt in a long time.

"I tried to be a good wife."

"I know." Mama's voice was soothing.

Grace hiccuped. "I really wanted to have a baby."

"Of course you did."

Sometime later, when the tears finally subsided, Grace lifted her head and looked at her mother in a new light. She hadn't given the woman enough credit. Mama really did love her.

Cupping Grace's tear-streaked cheeks, Mama said, "What did that ex-son-in-law of mine do this time?"

"He wants to sell our house."

"But you don't want to?"

"It's not that I don't want to." She sniffed, accepting the tissue Mama handed her. "I mean, I have no need for it anymore. It's just—" The turmoil that had been smoldering inside her ever since Aaron's call burst into flame.

Fists balled, she shot to her feet, rounded the solid wood coffee table and started to pace. "That was supposed to be my house." She poked a finger at her chest. "The place where I'd spend the rest of my days, where we'd raise our kids and welcome our grandkids." She faced her mother. "Now he expects me to sign some stupid piece of paper so he and wife 2.0 can buy a new house." Tears threatened again and her cheeks burned. "It's *not* fair."

Her mother sat calmly on the sofa, shaking her head. "No. It's not fair. But, baby, it doesn't do us any good to be angry about it either." Standing, she moved toward Grace. "We have to make a conscious choice to put it behind us and move on."

"I thought I'd done that."

"Are you sure?"

She looked curiously at her mother. "What are you getting at?"

Mama slipped an arm around Grace's waist, pulling her against her hip. "There's a difference between moving on and running away. Grace, don't let Aaron's actions rob you of the happiness you deserve. Someday Mr. Right will come along and—"

Grace pulled away. "Don't go there, Mama. Please. Even if there was a Mr. Right, I will never be Mrs. Right."

"Now, why would you say that? You're young, beautiful—"

"And broken." She flopped back down on the sofa. "No man wants a woman who can't give him children."

Mama's gaze narrowed as she returned to the couch. "Did a doctor tell you that you can't conceive?"

"No. But after trying unsuccessfully for two years, it's pretty obvious that God doesn't want me to have children."

"First of all—" her mother's expression softened "—even if you weren't able to conceive, that doesn't mean you can't have a family. And second, perhaps God simply didn't want you to have children with Aaron."

Grace snagged the pale blue throw pillow beside her and fiddled with the fringe. "Why would God not want me to have children with my husband? The man I vowed to love, honor and cherish until we were parted by death."

"God knows everything about us, Grace. You, me... Aaron." Conviction sparkled in Mama's hazel eyes. "Have you ever stopped to think that maybe He was protecting you?"

"Protecting me from what?"

Mama looked away briefly, as though she were afraid to say what was really on her mind. "I shouldn't try to speak for God. However, I can tell you this. I know what it is to feel broken. And even though I tried to run away, God still met me in my deepest pain."

"When Daddy died?"

Mama nodded. "I felt as though I'd died, too." Her eyes shimmered with unshed tears. "All the hopes and plans for our future were gone. I was all alone. And I was *so* angry." She reached for a tissue on the side table. Dabbed the tears that now streamed down her cheeks.

Grace watched her mother, wanting to comfort her, but unsure how. Finally, she laid a hand on Mama's knee.

Mama covered it with her own. "I tried to carry on. Went through the motions of day-to-day life, but it always felt as though there was this…tremendous weight on my shoulders."

Grace knew all too well what that felt like.

"One day, I couldn't take it anymore. I'd had enough. I went into my bedroom, dropped to my knees and gave God a piece of my mind."

"Really? What did you say?"

"Through gritted teeth, I said, *I can't do this. I don't want to do this.*" Tilting her head, her mother seemed to ponder the memory. Then the corners of her mouth lifted. "And you know what?"

"What?"

"In that still moment, I realized that wasn't what God was asking of me at all. Instead, He was holding out His hands, waiting for me to give it to Him. My pain, my worries and fears…" Mama shrugged. "So I did. Which is what I should have done in the first place."

She made it sound so simple.

"And did He take away the pain?"

"Not right away. I still had to walk that road, but I wasn't alone. And just like any wound, it healed over time."

She took both of Grace's hands in hers. "My precious

daughter, I've loved you your whole life. But God loves you so much more than either your father or I ever could. And I promise you, God's got more in store for you than you could ever imagine. But you have to let go of your anger. Give it to God and just see what He can do."

She appreciated what Mama was saying. But Grace had been running for so long and allowed the chasm between her and God to grow so deep... "I don't know if I can."

Chapter Ten

Dusk had fallen over Ouray by the time Grace was ready to leave her mother's. Talking things over with Mama had been easier than she'd imagined and she was glad they'd crossed paths. In her heart, Grace knew it was no coincidence, but she wasn't willing to acknowledge it as anything else just yet.

"You're sure you don't want to stay here tonight?" Mama followed her out onto the porch.

"I'm sure."

"I could drive or walk you back to your campsite."

"No, thanks, Mama. I have a lot I need to sort out, so it might be best if I'm alone."

"Will you check in with me tomorrow? Let me know how you're doing?"

Grace adjusted the pack on her shoulder. "I will. Thank you." She hugged her mother. "You were just what I needed tonight."

Tears filled Mama's eyes when they parted. She cupped Grace's cheek. "You don't know how much it pleases me to hear you say that."

Grace turned away before she started crying herself. "Night, Mama. I love you."

"I love you, too, Grace."

With the glow of the porch light fading behind her, Grace dabbed her eyes, trying to remember the last time she'd told her mother she loved her. And even when it had come, in phone calls or such, Mama was always the initiator. But she'd learned a lot about her mother since coming to Ouray. Enough to realize that, perhaps, they weren't so different after all.

Between Fifth and Sixth Avenues, Grace heard noises behind her. The crunching of gravel. Footfalls. Rapid footfalls. Though some sounded slightly different than the others.

At the sound of heavy breathing, she quickened her pace, daring a glance behind her.

A tall figure jogged along the street. Her momentary angst eased as she took in the basketball shorts, sleeveless T-shirt and—prosthetic?

"Grace?" Kaleb continued toward her, stopping in front of her. "What are you doing here? I thought you'd be fast asleep by now."

"Uh—" It wasn't just his question that gave her pause. Instead it was the rapid rise and fall of his muscular chest and that sweaty gray T that not only exposed his massive biceps, but the burn scars that spread up his left arm. Lowering her gaze, she eyed the bladelike prosthetic. "You run?"

Hands on his hips, his smile was slow. "And ski and just about everything else I did before the accident." He moved closer, his smile evaporating as he studied her face. "Have you been crying?"

She immediately turned away. She could only imagine what she must look like. Red-rimmed eyes, tear-streaked cheeks…

Drawing closer yet, he said, "Talk to me, Grace. Something's been bothering you for a couple days now. I don't like to see you hurting."

Hurting? How did he know she was hurting?

The concern in his eyes had her looking everywhere but at him. While she was fine with getting him to talk about his issues and pointing out in no uncertain terms where he was wrong, she was used to keeping things to herself. Why bother sharing when the person doing the asking really didn't care?

But Kaleb wasn't Aaron. He genuinely cared about people. Including her.

And, she supposed, there was one thing she needed to set the record straight on.

"Remember Memorial Day, when I followed you into the garage after the incident with Jack?"

He nodded, his gaze still boring into her.

"I led you to believe that I was some strong Christian woman when, actually, I'm kind of on the outs with God right now."

His brow shot up. "You're on the outs with Him or He's on the outs with you?"

She let go a sigh. "Probably the latter."

After examining her for another moment or two, he crossed his arms over his hulking chest. "So why are you mad at God?"

How did he come up with that? "Did I say I was mad at Him?"

"No. I inferred it."

"Oh." Taking a sudden interest in the dim streetlight overhead, she struggled for a response.

"Are you mad at Him?"

She dared to look at him again. "Let's just say He allowed a lot of things to happen in my life that I'm not real crazy about."

Kaleb chuckled as he hiked up the left leg of his shorts. "Are you sure you want to go there with me?"

She narrowed her gaze. "My wounds may not have been physical, but I have plenty of scars."

"I'm sorry. That was rather callous of me." He hesitated a moment. "Don't suppose you'd care to share, would you?"

"Not particularly." Her gaze fell. She wasn't good at sharing.

"You sure?" He scanned the stars that illuminated the night sky. "Nice night for a campfire."

She smiled, recalling that night they'd first started going through his military stuff. She'd pushed him relentlessly until he finally told her what his problem was. And then she went off on him and stormed away.

Yet it was Kaleb who'd apologized the next day, because he finally understood what she had been trying to make him see.

"Throw in a Diet Dr Pepper and you've got a deal."

A short time later, flames danced in the small fire pit at her campsite.

Night sounds echoed around them as she popped the top on her soda. She sat beside Kaleb at the picnic table, grateful that the campsites on either side of her were still empty. "That package that came for me today. It was from my ex-husband."

Something flashed in Kaleb's eyes, though she wasn't about to guess what it was. "I wasn't aware that you were married."

"A little over four years."

"So what happened?" With his back against the table, he stretched his legs out in front of him, as though settling in for a long story.

She took a deep breath, wondering where to start and just how much to say.

"Of course, you don't have to tell me, if you don't want to."

The fact that Kaleb was willing to let her off the hook encouraged her to continue. "Aaron and I tried for two years to have a baby." She fingered the water droplets on the outside of the soda can she'd set atop the table. "But I couldn't get pregnant. So, while I was out to sea, my husband went looking for someone who could."

Watching Kaleb, she saw his left eye twitch. His jaw squaring as the muscles tensed.

"Nothing like coming home from a ten-month deployment to news that your husband wants a divorce because his girlfriend is pregnant." She couldn't have stopped the sarcasm in her tone if she tried.

"That's rough." Raking a hand through his still-damp hair, he blew out a long, slow breath. "Sounds like your ex-husband was a real piece of work."

That wasn't exactly how she'd put it. "I'm just ashamed that it took me so long to realize it."

He turned, brushing the stray hairs away from her face. "Grace, you have nothing to be ashamed of. After what he did, Aaron is the one who ought to be ashamed."

"I know. But I still heard the whispers, saw the sympathetic stares."

"Believe me, I know all about those."

She contemplated him for a moment. "Yeah, I'm sure you do."

He took hold of her hand, as if offering his strength. "Mind if I ask what was in the package?"

She told him about the house and the document her ex needed her to sign.

Kaleb shook his head. "For the life of me, I don't understand how some people can be so heartless. You didn't deserve to be treated like that, Grace. Especially by your husband. He vowed to love, honor and cherish you." His gray-green eyes bored into hers. "You deserve to be cherished, Grace."

The intensity of both his words and his gaze had her pushing to her feet to stand beside the fire. "Now you know all about me and my baggage. However, after venting to my mother tonight, I am happy to say that I have signed the document without the least bit of remorse and am eager to move on with my life."

Kaleb stood. "And what about God? Is He still on the outs?"

Her shoulders sagged. "I haven't decided yet. Right now, He seems pretty distant."

"He hasn't moved, Grace. He's right where He's always been, waiting with open arms for you to return."

"I know. I'm sure I'll find my way back eventually. I'm just too weary, perhaps embarrassed, to make that journey right now."

"I understand. I've been there." Touching a finger to her chin, he forced her to look at him. "And I can tell you from experience that no matter how tough the journey may be, it's all worth it." He caressed her cheek, sending chill bumps down her spine. "What Aaron did was wrong. But don't let him steal your joy. You deserve to be happy, Grace."

Seeing the depth of sincerity in Kaleb's eyes, she realized that he was the kind of man who could do just that. A thought that was as comforting as it was disconcerting.

Good thing she was leaving at the end of the summer.

Or maybe not.

By early Saturday evening, Kaleb wasn't any more enthusiastic about gathering things for the museum than he was before. However, he was determined. He'd made a promise and he prided himself on being a man of his word. No matter how difficult it might be.

At least Grace would be there to help him.

"You ready to go?" He smiled at her across the office.

Behind the counter, she hoisted her pack onto her shoulder. "Yep. Pizza's ordered, so I think we're good to go."

Just the thought of spending time with her brought a smile to his face.

In the few weeks that they'd known each other they'd learned more than most people would over the course of months. It was as though there was some unseen connection between him and Grace. They simply got each other in a way no one else could. Something he found heartening and terrifying at the same time.

And after hearing what her ex had put her through, Kaleb's desire to protect her had grown even stronger.

"Better batten down your hatches." He opened the front door to an onslaught of wind and rain. "Go, go, go." He rushed Grace out the door and toward his Jeep as he locked the office behind him.

He hurried after her, throwing himself behind the steering wheel. "This is nuts. Reminds me of monsoon season."

"Monsoon season?" She eyed him across the center console.

"It's a weather pattern we usually go through from July to September."

She continued to stare at him. "A monsoon? In southwest Colorado?"

"Sounds crazy, I know." He fired up the engine before glancing her way. "You still want to help me tonight?"

"Better than weathering this out in my camper." She turned toward him, the corners of her mouth tilted upward. "However, I wouldn't mind checking on it."

He turned on the windshield wipers and shifted the Jeep into gear. "I hear you loud and clear."

Arriving at Grace's campsite, they saw that the tarp he'd helped her with a couple of weeks ago had come loose on one side and was flapping wildly in the wind. They quickly got out and attacked the problem, cinching the rope until everything was secure.

After retrieving the insulated jacket he'd loaned her from her camper, Grace dived into the Jeep alongside him, slamming the door behind her. "Monsoons, huh? Does this mean you're prone to hurricanes, too?" She shoved her arms into the sleeves of the coat.

"Not that I'm aware of." He adjusted the air from cool to heat and turned on the defroster to remove the fog from the windows. "Sure is raining enough, though."

"I'll say." She leaned back against the seat as he again hit the road.

After stopping to pick up their pizza, he headed straight for his house. Times like this he hated not having a garage. "Looks like we're going to have to make a run for it."

She lifted her pack over her head. "I'm ready."

"Isn't your computer in there?"

"Yes. But it's a waterproof bag."

He held up the pizza. "And what about this?"

She reached for the door handle. "Guard it with your life, soldier." Bailing from the vehicle, she sprinted for the front porch.

Donning a raincoat he found tucked in the backseat, he followed her at a brisk pace. "I usually use the back door."

A grin carved that dimple into her right cheek. "But there's no cover there." She eyed the roof that stretched the expanse of the porch.

"Good point." He opened the screen, shoved his key into the lock and held the door open for her.

Inside, he tossed the raincoat aside and set the pizza on the coffee table. "I'll be right back." He made his way down the hall to the linen closet and grabbed two towels. "Here you go." He pitched one her way when he returned to the living room.

"Thanks." She toweled her face first, then her hair before shrugging out of his old coat.

Continuing on into the kitchen, he grabbed a roll of paper towels. "What would you like to drink?"

"Got any Diet Dr—"

He'd meant to buy some. "Sorry. How about water?"

"That'll work."

By the time he returned, she was digging through one of the boxes he'd hauled into the living room and attempted to tackle the other night. Only to leave it untouched beside the coffee table.

"This would be great for the exhibit." She held up a zip-topped bag of Middle Eastern currency.

"I hadn't thought about it, but I guess you're right." He handed her a bottle of water.

With the water in one hand, she turned the bag with the other for a better look. "I know I'm right. People love this sort of stuff." She laid it on the table then twisted off the lid of the water bottle to take a drink.

He offered up a quick prayer before taking his favorite spot on the sofa and lifting the lid on the pizza box. He picked up a slice and was just about to take a bite when Grace cleared her throat.

He looked up at her. "Yes?"

"Don't get too comfortable. We still have work to do." She grabbed her own slice while rummaging through the box with her free hand.

Several slices later, both boxes sat empty.

Grace rolled up the sleeves of her plaid button-down

shirt. "One down, a dozen or so to go." The spunk in her hazel eyes when she glanced at him made him feel as though he were on a carnival ride. One that dipped, twisted and turned at warp speed. "You ready?"

"Ready as I'll ever be." He pushed himself off the couch. "Sounds like the winds might be dying down." He flipped on the light in the hall as they continued.

"Yeah, it does." She fell in line beside him. "That'll make my sleep experience a better one."

Reaching around the corner into the spare bedroom-turned-storage room, he located the light switch and flipped it on.

"What's that sound?" Grace looked at him curiously.

"I don't know."

Grace's sharp intake of breath echoed his own. "What happened?"

Something that looked like a pile of dirt sat just inside the door while water rained down from a two-by-three-foot hole in the ceiling.

Stepping into the room, he studied what could only be described as a disaster. He eyed the wet Sheetrock as he peered into the attic. Only then did he realize that what he thought was dirt was actually insulation.

"Oh, no. The boxes." Without a second thought, Grace charged into the room and scooped the nearest box into her arms.

Somewhat dazed, he watched as she scurried down the hall and deposited it in the living room before moving toward him again.

"Don't just stand there." She sent him her fiercest look. "Grab a box."

"Oh. Yeah." He rushed in behind her and armed himself with two containers. He passed Grace in the hall.

She was carrying the towels they'd used earlier. "What are those for?"

"The floor," she hollered over her shoulder. "Those old hardwoods don't take kindly to water."

More than an hour later, they collapsed, breathless, onto the sofa.

"Well...that was not how I'd planned to spend this evening." He absently massaged his left thigh where his stump and prosthetic met. It ached from all the back and forth.

"Me either." Grace huffed and puffed beside him.

He eyed the stack of boxes now in the corner of his living room. "We make a pretty good team."

Rolling her head to face him, she sent him an incredulous look. "You're just now figuring that out?"

"No. I'm just now stating it."

"Oh."

They sat in silence for a time, collecting their thoughts as well as catching their breath.

"Kaleb?" With one arm draped across her stomach, she stared at the ceiling.

"What?"

"You hear that?"

"Hear what?" He didn't hear anything.

"I think it stopped raining."

Standing, he moved to the front door. Opened it. "You're right." He stepped onto the porch, the rain-cooled air chilling his sweat-dampened skin.

Grace joined him, rubbing her arms. "It smells so clean out here. Earthy."

He leaned against the railing. "Thank you for helping me tonight. Sorry it didn't turn out the way we'd planned."

"I'm just glad we were here to discover what had happened. And that that pile of...whatever landed on the floor and not the boxes."

"Insulation."

"What?" She looked at him as if he were crazy.

"That pile. I'm pretty sure it was insulation."

"But it was black."

He shrugged. "Somehow the rain got into the attic, soaking the insulation, which, in turn, soaked the drywall, weakening it, and then the weight of the wet insulation caused it to cave in."

"I thought insulation was pink."

"Not in a hundred-year-old home."

"Eww." She looked so cute the way she scrunched up her nose.

He couldn't help laughing. "I'll call my insurance agent tomorrow."

"On a Sunday?"

"Good point. I'll just talk to him at church." He pushed away from the railing. "I'm sorry I wasted your time tonight, Grace."

"Wasted my time? Oh, you mean as opposed to me hanging out inside my camper all night to escape the rain?"

"In that case, I'm glad I could provide a little excitement." His boot scuffed against the wooden porch planks. "Still, we didn't accomplish much."

"We have one item."

He jerked his gaze to hers. "We do?"

"The money?"

"Oh, yeah. I forgot about that." He was procrastinating now. For whatever reason, he didn't want Grace to leave. Standing in front of her, he continued. "Thank you for helping me, Grace. You pitched right in. You were a real trooper."

Even in the dim lighting he could see the blush that crept into her cheeks as she looked up at him. "Nah, just a reformed petty officer. When water is involved, my instincts kick in."

"Either way, I appreciate it."

"You're welcome."

He stared down at her, wanting nothing more than to take her into his arms and hold her close. To run his fingers through her hair and feel its softness. To taste the sweetness of her lips.

Raking a hand through his hair, he turned away. "It's time to get you home."

A while later, as he watched her disappear into her camper, he pondered what it would be like to have someone like Grace at his side all the time. A partner. A helper. Someone he could walk through life with, knowing that if he stumbled, they wouldn't let him fall.

Grace was that kind of woman. But, come September, she'd be gone. And he didn't have a clue what he'd do without her.

Chapter Eleven

A shopping trip in Montrose with Mama Sunday afternoon was an unexpected treat. And considering Grace's all-too-basic wardrobe, one she intended to take full advantage of.

"What about this one?" Mama held up a silky turquoise tank top. "It would look beautiful on you."

Grace fingered the delicate material. "You don't think it's too dressy?"

"Not at all. This would go great with jeans, shorts, a skirt…just about anything."

Since Grace didn't have a lot of fashion sense, she appreciated her mother's flair for style. "Okay, I'll try it."

Grace continued to peruse a rack of shirts, amazed at how much lighter she felt since talking with her mother and Kaleb a few days ago. It was as though a burden the size of an aircraft carrier had been lifted from her shoulders.

A part of her wondered if by not signing over her portion of the house before she left Jacksonville, it allowed Aaron some invisible hold over her. But in her heart, she knew it was because she had finally acknowledged her bitterness toward God. And while she still had a long road back to a fully restored relationship, she was at least talking to Him again, if only to voice her displeasure.

"This is cute." She showed her mother a deep burgundy T-shirt with black and silver embellishments, grateful that God had reconciled them. After Daddy died, Grace was so wrapped up in her own grief that she failed to consider how much Mama must have been hurting. For that, she was ashamed. Mama had lost her best friend and the only man she'd ever loved. And Mama had stayed by his side until the very end.

"Oh, yes. Very nice."

After Daddy's funeral, Grace went back to Florida and Lucy returned to school, leaving Mama to pick up the pieces of her broken heart all by herself. The realization had Grace thanking God for bringing Roger and Mama together. From now on, she would judge Roger for the man he was, not the man she believed him to be.

Standing on opposite sides of the rack, they continued to flip through hangers.

"So have you and Kaleb made much headway for the museum?"

"A little." Grace slid one shirt after another from right to left. "But that leak in his roof kind of stopped us in our tracks."

"Has it been difficult for him? Going through all those memories."

"Yeah." Grace picked up a tangerine tunic, then put it back. "The first night was really tough on him."

"Oh, I hate that this is causing him pain. We want this event to be touching, but we also want it to be uplifting."

"I know that. And I think he knows that." She contemplated what Kaleb had said about blaming himself, but wasn't about to share something so personal. "Still, there's a lot of stuff in there that puts him face-to-face with the friends he lost." She approached her mother, who was holding an armload of clothes. "Okay. I think I'm ready to try—"

Mama grimaced momentarily, holding a hand to her chest.

"Are you okay?" Grace stepped closer.

"Yeah." Mama waved her off. "Just a little indigestion, that's all."

"Are you sure? Do you need anything?"

"I'm fine, baby." She handed the clothing to Grace. "You go try these on. And don't forget to come out and model for me." Just like when Grace was little. But she didn't mind. Matter of fact, she was actually kind of enjoying shopping for a change.

"I'll be out in a sec." Inside the dressing room, she tried on the red-and-black T first. Yuck. The colors were fine, but the style did not fit her at all. Better let Mama have the last word, though.

She strolled out of the dressing room.

"It's...okay." Her mother cocked her head this way and that.

"No worries, Mama. I don't like it either."

The woman looked relieved. "Okay, good."

Next one. The turquoise tank. She slipped it over her head. Looked in the mirror. Yep, this one was a keeper.

Again, she headed into the store. "Mama?" Her mother was slumped against the wall, seemingly struggling for each breath. Grace rushed to her side. "Tell me what's wrong, Mama."

"I—I—" She gasped for air. "My chest. Hard to—"

Tugging the cell phone from her back pocket, Grace dialed 911.

"9-1-1, please state your emergency."

"It's my mom. I think she's having a heart attack."

Grace swallowed the lump in her throat. She'd already lost one parent. She was too young to lose another. Not now. Especially not now. She and Mama were finally forming a bond. "We're at Avery's Style Mart. Hurry. Please."

By the time the paramedics arrived, Mama was whiter than Grace had ever seen her. Grace clung to the woman's hand. "I'm right here, Mama. I'm right here."

Roger.

He'd taken out a tour today. She glanced at her watch. Three o'clock. He probably wouldn't be back for another hour.

While the paramedics evaluated her mother, she dialed his cell phone. No answer.

Not knowing what to do, she dialed Kaleb. "I need your help."

"What's going on?"

"I don't know, but I think Mama might be having a heart attack. I need to let Roger know."

"Where are you?"

"We're in Montrose. I don't know. Do they have a hospital here?"

"Yeah. A good one, too. She'll be in good hands."

She could feel tears stinging the backs of her eyes. "Tell Roger to hurry."

"Grace?"

"Yes?"

"God's got this, all right. I'm praying for both Donna and you. You just stay calm and be there for your mama."

A sob caught in her throat as they loaded Mama onto the gurney. "I will."

Grabbing her mother's purse, she followed as they wheeled Mama to the ambulance.

"Miss? Oh, miss."

Grace turned to see a clerk trotting behind her.

"The shirt. I'm sorry, but you'll have to pay for it."

She glanced at the price tag, grabbed a wad of bills from the back pocket of her jeans and handed a twenty and ten to the clerk. "Keep the change."

"Will you be following us?" The female paramedic looked back at her as they loaded Mama into the ambulance.

"No." Still holding her mother's red cross-body purse, she climbed up behind them. "I'm coming with you."

With sirens wailing, they set off for the hospital.

Inside the ambulance, they started an IV on her mother, as well as an EKG. Before they could do any more, they arrived at the hospital.

Grace couldn't remember her heart ever beating so wildly.

As they opened the back doors of the ambulance, her mother looked at her. Behind the oxygen mask, Grace saw a look of fear. One that seemed to say, "Don't leave me."

She was pretty scared herself. But she had to stay strong. "I'm still here, Mama." She reached for her hand. The woman grabbed hold and Grace squeezed.

Then they pulled the gurney from the vehicle, breaking the connection.

Grace followed as they rushed through the automatic doors, into the emergency room.

"Female, age fifty-nine," one paramedic rattled off. "Possible heart attack."

She looked down at her mother. Though she didn't think it possible, her mother had grown even more ashen. "We're here, Mama. We're at the hospital. They're going to take good care of you."

They rushed through another set of doors, then made a quick left into a triage room.

Fluorescent lights glared overhead as they transferred Mama to the hospital bed. Nurses pulled on blue exam gloves and hurried to connect monitors.

"BP is one-sixty over ninety," said another paramedic. "Heart rate one-ten."

The flurry of activity had Grace pressing her back against the wall. She didn't like feeling so helpless. But what could she do?

Pray.

Pray? That was something she hadn't done in a long time. Okay, so she was talking to God again. But praying? That involved faith. Believing that God might actually do what you were asking.

There was a time when she believed God heard her prayers. That He interceded on her behalf. But now? Did she trust God to help Mama?

A tiny spark somewhere deep inside her told her that she could. But she'd have to choose to believe.

God, I know You're there. And I know that You know what's going on down here. Please be with Mama. Comfort her and protect her. She drew in a shaky breath. *God, I can't lose her. I wasted so many years being angry with her.* She swallowed hard. *And You. Forgive me. Please.*

Lucy. Grace needed to call her. No, she'd wait until she had some news. And then face her sister's wrath. Lucy would have a cow if she knew Grace hadn't called her immediately.

Pulling out her phone, she moved just outside the door where she could still see and hear everything that was going on.

"Hey, Grace. What's going on?"

"I'm in the emergency room. With Mama."

"Oh, no! What's wrong?"

"We just got here, so I don't have any details, but she might have had a heart attack."

"A heart attack? Mama?" Lucy's voice quivered. "This can't be happening." Grace imagined her sister shoving her fingers through her long blond hair. "We can't lose her, too, Grace."

"I'm not about to let that happen, Luce. I need to go now, but I promise I'll call you back just as soon as I know something."

"Okay. Thanks, Grace."

"Mrs. Hamilton, do you have any allergies?" she heard one of the nurses ask as she reentered Mama's room.

Did Grace even know the answer to that?

The nurse punched the information into a computer.

"Do you have a DNR?" Why did the nurse continue to badger her mother? Couldn't they see she was struggling just to breathe, let alone talk?

"Thank you." The nurse returned to her computer.

Grace resumed her post at the wall. Watching her mother, a woman so full of life, suddenly forced to fight for it, shook Grace to the core. She battled the tears that begged to be unleashed. But she would not give in. At least not when her mother could see her. She had to stay strong. Something she should be good at by now. Instead, she felt as though she could crumble at any moment.

God, I'll do whatever You want. Just, please, don't take Mama.

Roger was visibly shaken when Kaleb gave him the news about Donna. So there was no way Kaleb was going to let him drive all the way to Montrose. Better to close a couple of hours early than risk his friend's life.

Besides, he wanted to be there for Grace. When he'd talked with her on the phone, he could tell she was struggling. And given that she'd been the calm in more than a few of his storms lately, it was time to return the favor.

By the time he and Roger arrived at the hospital, doctors had determined that Donna had not had a heart attack. Unfortunately, they feared she may have a blockage, and she was undergoing a heart catheterization when they finally located Grace in the waiting room.

She stood, her expression hovering between worry and relief. Enduring something like this was never easy, but it was even tougher when you had to face it alone. "Glad you guys finally made it."

"Me, too," said Roger. "Any word?"

"No." Her arms were crossed over her chest. "They said someone would be out to talk to us once the procedure is over."

"Guess all we can do is wait, then." Roger raked a hand through his gray hair, leaving it standing on end.

Kaleb could only imagine what was going through his head. After all, he'd already buried one wife. Donna was his second chance. And Roger loved her with every fiber of his being, just as he had Camille.

While Roger paced, Kaleb kept his focus on Grace. He could see the fear in the depth of her hazel eyes. "How are you doing?"

She shrugged. "As well as can be expected, I guess." The nonchalance of her response gave him pause.

He'd heard the angst in her voice when she called him earlier. The fear of losing another parent had threaded every word.

Now she was shutting him out. Closing the door on her emotions and mentally retreating to that place where no one or nothing could hurt her.

And it stung. He'd revealed so much to Grace. Taking

her to some of his darkest places. And yet she still refused to trust him.

A man dressed in blue scrubs pushed through the door then.

Roger and Kaleb flanked Grace as the doctor continued toward them.

His gaze traveled to Roger. "Are you Mr. Hamilton?"

"Yes, sir."

"Dr. Griffith." The man shook Roger's hand before addressing them collectively. "Mrs. Hamilton had significant blockages in her coronary arteries. We were, however, able to insert stents into both, so she should be ready to go home by tomorrow."

Grace and Roger both let go a sigh of relief.

"When can we see her?" Roger watched the other man intently.

"Only one of you will be able to join her in recovery. The nurse will let you know when they're ready for you."

As the doctor left, Grace turned to Roger. "Mama will be eager to see you."

Roger let go a sigh, shoving his hands into the pockets of his jeans. "I'm pretty eager to see her myself."

"I know you are." Grace squared her shoulders. "I can see her later."

She was putting on quite the act. But Kaleb had glimpsed behind the mask. He knew the tender heart that lay behind the tough facade. So for now, let her walk that tightrope. However, he'd also make sure that he was there to catch her when she fell.

"Kaleb?" Roger looked past Grace. "Would you mind running Grace to pick up Donna's SUV?"

"Not at all."

When he and Grace exited the hospital thirty minutes later, the sun hovered over the western horizon.

She walked through the parking lot in silence, her arms wrapped around her middle as though she were fighting to keep her emotions from escaping.

Placing his hand against the small of her back, he urged her around to the passenger side of his Jeep. For a moment, he felt her trembling. Before she jerked away.

"Grace?" He stepped in front of her, hoping she might relax and let down her guard. But when she refused to look at him, he continued. "Where are we going?"

"Avery's something."

"Ah, Avery's Style Mart." He opened the door. "Hop in."

The round-trip took all of twenty minutes. And though she tried to evade him, parking on the opposite side of the parking lot, he caught up to her on their way into the hospital.

"What are your plans for tonight?" He followed her through the automatic door. "Are you going to stay here or do you want me to take you back to Ouray?"

She continued across the shiny tile. "I think it's best if I stay here with Mama."

Why did he get the feeling she'd been rehearsing her response. "I'm sure Roger will want to stay, too."

She pushed the up button on the elevator. "Then I'll sleep in the waiting room if I have to." Stubbornness squared her shoulders.

How much longer could she go on like this? At some point, she was going to break.

Nonetheless, he said, "Whatever you like."

He waited with Roger while Grace went in to see her mother. "How was Donna?"

"She's resting comfortably." Forearms on his thighs, his friend rubbed his hands together. "Boy, you talk about a sight for sore eyes."

Roger was a blessed man. To find love twice. Kaleb had

yet to have a relationship that even resembled that kind of love. Though he wasn't about to give up hope.

When Grace rejoined them, Roger presented her with a set of keys. "Could I get you to check on the house for us?"

The conflicted expression on Grace's face had Kaleb biting back a laugh. So much for staying at the hospital.

"Oh." She tentatively took hold of the keys. "Um… sure."

"You don't mind driving her back to Ouray, do you, Kaleb?"

"No, of course not." Though he could guarantee that Grace wasn't too excited about the prospect.

"I appreciate it." Roger smiled at Grace. "You're welcome to stay there, if you like."

"Uh, yeah… Thank you." Her gaze fell to the tan carpet.

Though Kaleb had no doubt that Grace wanted to be with her mother, he also knew she'd be better off getting a good night's rest. Something that was not easily accomplished in a hospital. Besides, Roger would call if anything were to happen.

Kaleb touched her elbow. "It'll be dark soon, so we should get going."

She reluctantly acquiesced.

"Shall we grab a bite to eat?" He motioned to a fast-food place on their way out of Montrose.

"I'm not hungry." Grace stared out the window, continuing to do so until they pulled up in front of Roger and Donna's darkened house thirty minutes later.

She quickly jumped out.

Kaleb killed the engine and followed her. "Looks like everything's off to me."

"I'd better make sure." Grace continued up the front steps.

She unlocked the door and went inside. Once she'd

turned on a lamp or two, Kaleb stepped just inside the front door. "Check the kitchen."

A moment later, she returned. "It's fine. I'll check upstairs." She disappeared for a short time and he heard floorboards creaking overhead. Then she made her way back down the steps. "Everything's fine."

If only that were true.

"Okay, good." But Grace was far from fine. He watched her as she hesitated at the foot of the stairs. "What's going on, Grace? Why are you shutting down on me?"

She immediately crossed her arms over her chest, her feet riveted to the hardwood floor. "Shutting down? What do you mean?"

He moved closer. "Let it go, Grace. We both know you're hurting."

Though she refused to look at him, he saw her bottom lip quiver. She was fighting hard to keep it together.

"You're not as tough as you pretend to be." He continued toward her. "You're afraid of losing the only parent you have left." The words sounded harsh, even to his own ears. But he had to get through to her.

Her liquid eyes looked everywhere but at him. Her shoulders drooped.

Erasing what little space remained between them, he pulled her to him and enveloped her in his embrace.

Instead of objecting, she wrapped her arms around him, sobs racking her body.

He caressed her hair. "It's okay, Grace. You're safe. Let it go." He would hold her forever if she needed him to.

She fisted his shirt. "I was—" she hiccuped "—so scared. I can't lose her, too. I can't." Her words were muffled against his chest.

"I know. And you did great. You got your mom the

help she needed." He tightened his hold and simply allowed her to cry.

When she finished, she looked up at him, her eyes still shimmering with unshed tears. "Do you think she's going to be okay?"

"Yes, Grace, I believe your mother is going to be okay. But what about you?"

"I've been, um—" her gaze drifted to the ceiling and she blinked rapidly "—praying. A lot."

"That's good. Matter of fact, that's real good."

"How did Roger take it?" She tried to swipe away her tears. "When you told him."

"Not too well." He stroked her hair. "Like you, he's lost someone he loved very much. So a lot of those fears you had were going on inside of him, too. And the fact that he wasn't there only exacerbated things."

With his arms still around her, she nodded, her eyes never leaving his. The gold and green flecks that had diminished earlier were back. And more stunning than ever.

His heart pounded. He needed to get out of here. Take Grace back to her campsite before he did something he'd regret.

He released her. Took a step back. "We need to go."

"I was, um, thinking I'd stay here tonight."

Conflicted, he stared down at her. "Do you need to go get some clothes or anything?"

"No, I'll be all right."

"And what about tomorrow? You're welcome to take the day off, if you like."

She took a step closer. "I'll probably come in early and then go from there."

"That's fine."

For the longest while, they continued to stare at each other. His mouth went dry, his pulse racing like crazy.

"Grace?"

Her eyes were wide as she stared up at him. "Yes?"

Try as he might, he couldn't make himself look away. He didn't want to. All he wanted was to taste her lips.

Reaching for her, he lowered his head and did just that, as though it were the most natural thing in the world.

Best of all, she kissed him back. And he'd never tasted anything so sweet.

Wrapping both arms around her waist, he pulled her closer, deepening their kiss.

Grace threaded her fingers through the back of his hair. She smelled amazing. Like flowers and sunshine.

Then she tensed and pulled away, her eyes wide. "You should go."

His breathing was ragged. "I think you're right."

He turned for the door, raking a disgusted hand through his hair. What had he been thinking? Kissing her when she was at her most vulnerable.

She kissed you back.

Yeah, because she needed to be comforted. Not taken advantage of.

Hand on the storm door, he glanced over his shoulder. She remained where he'd left her, fingers pressed to her lips.

"Sleep well, Grace." Heart heavy, he stepped into the night. Though the timing of his kiss may have been off, there was one thing he now knew for certain.

He'd fallen for Grace.

Chapter Twelve

❧

Grace downed her second cup of coffee the next morning, then reached for a Diet Dr Pepper. After tossing and turning all night, she'd need all the caffeine she could get her hands on just to make it through the day.

After showering at Mama's, she'd come back to her campsite to change and get ready for work. Despite having a comfortable bed for a change, sleep was elusive. Worries about Mama had plagued her brain. She was beyond grateful that God had spared her mother. But she also prayed that they could have more time together.

And then there was that kiss.

Even now, her lips tingled at the thought. The warmth of Kaleb's embrace made her feel special and wanted. Yeah, she'd enjoyed it all right. Until she realized what a huge mistake she was making.

Inside her camper, she picked up a brush and ran it through her still-damp hair. She was only in Ouray for the summer. Kaleb knew that; she knew that. So kissing him was like playing with fire. And she'd be the one getting burned.

Her cell phone rang.

She tossed the brush aside and grabbed the phone from its charger.

Lucy. Probably looking for an update on Mama.

Grace had called her last night before turning in. Unfortunately, she hadn't spoken with Roger yet this morning, so she didn't have any more news.

"Hey, Luce."

"Any word on Mama?"

"Not yet." Holding the phone between her ear and shoulder, Grace pulled her hair back, gave it a couple of twists and affixed it to the back of her head with a claw clip.

"I figured, since I hadn't heard from you. Anyway, the main reason I'm calling is to let you know that I'm coming to Ouray."

She again took hold of the phone. "When?"

"I'm already on the road. Should be in sometime this afternoon."

"Mama will be glad to see you." However, she had to admit that she'd kind of enjoyed having her mother to herself. When Mama and Lucy were together, Grace couldn't seem to find a way to fit in.

"Ditto. I just wish it was under better circumstances. I'm so glad you were there for her, though. I mean, what if you'd been out on that cruise ship? How would we have gotten ahold of you?"

"I'm sure they have ways for you to contact me in case of emergency. How long are you planning to stay?" She glanced at her watch, then picked up her blush and swiped each cheekbone a couple of times.

"A few days. A week. Whatever it takes to help her get settled in once she comes home."

"If all goes according to plan, that should be today." She glanced at herself in a hand mirror. Rough, but it would have to do. "Hey, I'm late for work, Luce. I'll call you if I learn anything."

Ending the call, she took a deep breath. This was definitely going to be one of *those* days. Starting with having to face Kaleb. *God, please help me keep it together.*

Grabbing her pack, she set off for work, hoping to hear from Roger soon. With Mama coming home today, there was no point in Grace going to the hospital. If that changed, she'd catch a ride with Lucy later today.

Gravel crunched beneath her übercomfortable, though not-so-cute, sandals as she hiked up Seventh Avenue. The day had already been chaotic. And it was only a little past seven.

What if you'd been out on that cruise ship? Lucy's words replayed in her mind.

What if Mama hadn't been in Montrose when her breathing failed? She was only there because of Grace. If she'd been in Ouray, they'd have lost at least thirty minutes of valuable time.

And what if Grace were at sea? Did the cruise line have a plan for getting the crew home in case of emergencies? Surely they did. Though it would likely involve their next port of call. By then, it could be too late.

Arriving at Mountain View Tours, she shoved her thoughts aside and drew in a long, bolstering breath before going inside. *Nothing has changed, so just act normal.*

She hurried through the garage, offering a quick "Good morning" to Kaleb and five of his guides before moving inside. After dropping her pack behind the counter, she trashed her empty soda can, snagged a fresh one from the mini fridge and pulled the clipboards for this morning's tours before unlocking the front door.

Fortunately for her, Kaleb had volunteered to cover Roger's tours. That meant she wouldn't have to worry about being alone with him. It would also give her time to further rein in her flailing emotions, tie them in a tidy little bow and stuff them so deep they'd never have a chance to surface again.

The front door pushed open then and a young family entered, led by two energetic boys she remembered from Saturday. Somewhere around six and eight years old, both held small action figures and readily provided sound effects as the figures zoomed through the air, guided by the boys' small fingers.

A loud "Shooooom..." echoed through the air, followed by an explosive sound as one of the action figures careened toward the newly carpeted floor.

"Boys..." The father's warning went unheeded.

The garage door flew open then and Kaleb stepped inside. His commanding presence seemed to stop the boys in their tracks.

Buzz-cut heads tilted all the way back; mouths agape, they stared up at Kaleb.

"Looks like you fellas are having fun." Kaleb smiled down at them. "Are you ready to do some exploring today?"

The boys nodded as if in awe.

"All right. Well, you just hang tight for just a couple minutes." He shook both parents' hands. "Good to see you again."

He joined Grace behind the desk, glancing over the clipboards as he approached. "Lane's going to be taking Roger's tours."

Her gut tightened, her emotions fighting against the flimsy restraint she'd halfheartedly cinched around them. "So you'll—"

"Be here. Yes." He didn't sound any happier about the prospect than she was. And he had yet to look her in the eye. Obviously she wasn't the only one with regrets about last night. So how come his bugged her?

Once the tours departed, Grace didn't see hide or hair

of Kaleb. She had no doubt that he was hiding from her, trying to avoid any discussion about what had taken place last night.

Fine by her. She'd rather forget the whole incident. Or at least that was what she told herself. Yet images still crept into the forefront of her mind and she'd find herself wondering what it would be like to have the love of a man like Kaleb. A man who loved through actions and not just words. A man who knew what love really meant.

Shaking them away, she heard the garage door open. That could only mean—

"Grace, I think we need to talk."

She turned away from the computer and, for the first time today, allowed herself to look into Kaleb's handsome face. "About?"

"I think you know." Still standing a few feet from the counter, he removed his camo army ball cap and scratched a hand through his short hair before tugging the cap back into place. "I shouldn't have kissed you last night."

She lowered her gaze, not wanting to feel the stab of pain his words inflicted on her heart. Of course he shouldn't have kissed her. Now that he'd had time to think, he probably realized the error of his ways. After all, what man would want a woman who couldn't bear him children?

"Though I can't say that I'm sorry about it either. Just the timing. You were vulnerable, and I took advantage of that."

He thought she was vulnerable? When she'd wanted, practically initiated, that kiss?

She lifted her head as he moved closer.

"I like you, Grace." His smile was bashful and boyish, which only added to his charm. "I like you a lot. And, given the opportunity, I'd like to see where things could lead with us."

Us? What us? There was no *us*. She was leaving in September.

But he wants there to be.

She swallowed the sudden lump in her throat, not sure how she felt about what he'd just said. The part of her that could fall for Kaleb in a heartbeat wanted to run with the prospect. But the practical, been-burned-before part of her told her to keep her distance.

"I—uh…"

He lifted a palm to stop her. "It's okay. You don't have to say anything." Shoving his hands in the pockets of his medium wash jeans, he started toward the garage. "I just wanted to acknowledge the elephant in the room and let you know how I feel." With that, he shoved through the door and was gone.

So much for taking control of her emotions. They'd now broken loose and were running rampant. Some wanted to fist-pump the air, while others were ready to run and hide.

She'd never felt more conflicted. Imagining herself with Kaleb was so easy. But she'd been down that road before and the results were disastrous.

Besides, she had other commitments. Commitments that took her far away from Ouray.

Her gaze drifted to the window, taking in all that was small-town life. The flags that lined Main Street waving in the breeze, the old buildings painted in an array of colors and people stopping to chat on the street.

Oh, but Ouray wasn't just any small town. The mountains that enveloped it, along with their rich history, were the very essence of Ouray. Her focus lifted to the evergreen-blanketed slopes at the town's edge. The pioneering spirit may not have been born in Ouray, but it still thrived. In the month that she'd been here, she'd met person after person who had given up their homes, jobs and 401(k) plans in exchange for something more meaningful. Something fulfilling. No matter how hard they had to work.

Her phone rang, stirring her from her thoughts.

"Hey, Roger. How's Mama?" Little by little she was growing more comfortable with him. In no way, shape or form was he the opportunistic man she'd once imagined him to be.

"Better than expected. Her color is back to normal, she's breathing freely..."

Grace's heart swelled. "That is good news. Is she coming home today?"

"Yes."

"Oh, I'm so glad to hear it. Tell Mama that Lucy called and she's on her way up here for a few days."

"Donna will be happy about that. But, Grace, I was hoping... Well, would you reconsider staying with your mother and me for the rest of your time here in Ouray?"

A smile started somewhere in her heart, quickly moving to her face. She opened her mouth, but the words refused to come.

"You'll have your own bedroom, your own bathroom. You can come and go as you please. It would mean a lot to both of us."

Her bottom lip quivered as unbidden tears trailed down her cheeks. Despite all her rebellion and ornery antics, God had given her the desire of her heart.

"Thank you." She sniffed, feeling rather humbled. "I think I'd like that very much."

Wednesday evening, Kaleb could feel panic closing in. He eyed the boxes still stacked in his living room, his gut churning. He'd never make it by Saturday. At least not on his own. If he intended to get his stuff to the museum in time, he needed Grace's help.

He hated to ask her, though. She was dealing with her

own stuff. Her mother, moving… Not to mention what a fool he was for kissing her.

Still…

He at least had to give it a shot. If she said no, well, he'd figure that out if and when the time came.

Grabbing his car keys, he hurried outside, fired up his Jeep and headed the few blocks to Roger and Donna's.

What if Grace said no? Sure, things had been fine between them at work, but this wasn't work. He was selfishly asking her to do something out of the goodness of her heart. Not much different than that night he took advantage of her kiss.

But he wasn't taking advantage of Grace. At least, he didn't think so. He liked being with her. Valued her input. Trusted her enough to share his darkest secrets.

Shadows covered Ouray as he parked alongside the road and made his way up the front steps, glancing at the unfamiliar car in the drive. Must belong to Grace's sister.

The window was open on the storm door, so he could hear voices and the television through the screen.

With his heart beating erratically, he pressed the bell.

"Hey, buddy." Roger pushed open the door. "What's up?"

"Is Grace here?"

"No, she went over to her campsite to shut things down and bring her trailer back here." The older man stepped out onto the porch, wearing cargo shorts and a T-shirt. "I offered to go with her, but she insisted she could take care of it herself."

"That sounds like Grace." He thought back to that day she first arrived, when she had a flat tire. She was good at refusing help. Although he suspected it had more to do with looking after her mother this time than accepting help.

"Don't worry, Roger. I'll head on over there. See if I can't give her a hand." And, hopefully, vice versa.

Windows open, he took off across town. This week had brought them some fantastic weather with above-normal temps, which was good for business. Lord willing, the warm weather would also speed up the snowmelt in the higher elevations, allowing the county to get some of the passes there open earlier than usual.

Easing up to Grace's campsite, he saw that her camper was once again a tiny trailer and hitched to the back of her bike. He took a minute to admire it. Another time, another place...

Dressed in jeans and a gray United States Navy T-shirt, Grace lifted a footlocker onto the trailer's tongue.

He got out of the Jeep and started toward her. "Need some help?"

She blew at a stray hair that had escaped her clip to dangle in front of her face. "Little late, don't you think?"

He picked up the cooler. "I would have been happy to help, if somebody would have told me what they had planned."

"Yeah, yeah." She took hold of the cooler. "There are some bungee cords in my right saddlebag. Mind grabbing them for me?"

He did and handed them to her.

"Thanks." While she secured the items, he scanned the now vacant campsite, feeling a bit melancholy that she was leaving. Well, moving, anyway.

"Looks like you've got everything."

"Yep." She slipped her hands into her back pockets. "I'll settle up with Bud and Luann in the morning."

His gaze drifted to the fire pit, thinking about how integral it had been to their relationship. "I see you've got a few pieces of wood left." He glanced at Grace. "Shame to let it go to waste."

Eyes narrowing, she perched her hands on her hips. "You can't be serious."

"What? You know I love campfires."

She gestured to the three split logs. "There isn't enough wood to make a big fire."

"Who said anything about big?" He simply wanted to have her to himself for a little longer.

Shaking her head, she chuckled. "You're incorrigible."

"I've been called worse things." He gathered some twigs, tossed them into the pit. "So what do you say? I'll still make sure we get your trailer back."

"We?" She crossed her arms over her chest.

"Yes, we. I came with the intention of helping you and I intend to do just that. No matter how late I might be."

"How did you—"

"Would you mind handing me your lighter?" He'd seen it in her saddlebag.

Digging through his pockets, he pulled out a couple of receipts and tucked them beneath the kindling. "Have a seat." He gestured to the picnic table. "I'll be right with you."

She puffed out a laugh. "You're a mess, you know that?" She plopped down on the bench.

"That's me. An incorrigible mess." He lit the papers. Waited a few moments before blowing on the flame. "We've had some interesting conversations around this fire pit." As the flames spread, he added the larger twigs. "This'll be our last hurrah."

"Let's see." She touched a finger to her chin. "It was here that I pushed you to reveal your baggage and it's also where you pushed me to tell you mine. So what are we going to discuss this time?"

He laid the split logs on the fire before joining her. They sparked and flared to life. "I don't know. What baggage have you got left?"

Her genuine laughter was like rain on parched soil.

"I need your help, Grace. Saturday is the deadline to get my items to the museum. Yet, whenever I look at those boxes—"

"You're overwhelmed."

"Exactly." He let go a sigh. "Look, I know you've got your own life to deal with…"

"That's true. However, do you know how upset my mother would be if you failed to meet that deadline? She's convinced that your memorabilia is what's going to make this exhibit."

He stared at Grace. Donna upset? That was hard to imagine. Disappointed maybe. "We definitely can't have that."

"After what she's been through, no, we cannot. So, we've got to hit it and hit it hard. Tomorrow night, Friday night, even Saturday morning, if need be."

"Um…" Dumbfounded, he scratched his head. "Okay. Yeah. I'm willing to put forth whatever it takes."

"That means no more distractions, you got that?" She was beginning to sound like a drill instructor.

"You think I planned to have a leaky roof?"

"No. But no more steak dinners. Pizza is fine. Sandwiches. Anything we can eat with one hand."

"Works for me."

As daylight faded, he kept his focus on the flames, but held out his hand. "How are things going? I mean, with your sister here and all?"

Grace actually took hold. "Not too bad, I guess."

He sensed her hesitating. "But?"

She took a deep breath. Blew it out. "Tonight, at dinner, Lucy announced she was pregnant."

Ouch. "How do you feel about that?"

"I'm happy for her, of course. But she's only been married a little over a year." Grace lifted a shoulder. "It stings a little that she was able to achieve something I couldn't."

"Did Lucy know you had been trying to get pregnant?"

"No." Grace shook her head, then laid it against his arm. A move so subtle, yet one that seemed to validate his feelings.

"Grace?"

"Yeah."

"Just for the record, when I kissed you, I wasn't trying to take advantage of you."

Lifting her head, she looked at him as if he were crazy. "I know that." Her gaze seemed to search his. "In case you couldn't tell, I wanted you to kiss me."

"You did?" Hmm… Apparently his sensors were out of whack.

"I did." She let go of his hand. "And then I realized how selfish that was. I mean, I'm leaving in September. It's not like we could have any kind of long-term relationship or anything."

He halfway smiled. "I had the same thoughts." Although, it didn't stop him from wishing. And praying. "But we could definitely stay in contact. Through email and such."

"Absolutely."

The wind rustled the leaves overhead, filling the void. He scanned the darkening sky. "I suppose we should get you back to your folks." Eyeing the water spigot, he stood, knowing he'd need to douse the fire.

"Yeah." She pushed to her feet. "And then tomorrow night—"

"We hit the boxes and work to make your mama happy."

Chapter Thirteen

Grace grabbed another box Friday night and pulled open the flaps. They'd made a lot of progress last night, coming up with a few items. Though they still hadn't come across anything significant for the museum display. And at this rate, they might not.

On the other side of Kaleb's living room, he stood near the sofa sorting through stacks of photos. She was proud of him for his stick-to-itiveness. For pushing past whatever emotions he might be battling to get the job done. Because tomorrow they would be handing off whatever they came up with.

Peering into her box, she saw layers of wadded packing paper, unlike the others where stuff had just been tossed inside. She removed the paper to find another slightly smaller box with a lid.

"Any idea what might be in here?" She pulled out the smaller box and set it on top of another box.

"Not a clue." He was beside her now. "Shall we find out?"

She watched as he lifted the lid, realizing it was a hat-box of some sort.

Kaleb pulled out the tissue paper. "It's my helmet."

No doubt about that. Except this helmet had a pretty hefty dent in it and the pixelated camo cover was torn in multiple spots, as though it had been pelted repeatedly.

That was when it hit her. "Is this the helmet you were wearing when the IED went off?"

"Sure is." He pulled it from the box. "This thing probably saved my life." He fingered the dent.

Judging by the size and location of the spot... "I'm certain it did." A shudder ran through her. Though she'd heard the extent of Kaleb's injuries, this visual made her realize just how close he'd come to dying. And even though he was alive and well and standing beside her now, the thought still made her sad.

"Guess you didn't have to wear these in the navy." He looked from the helmet to her.

"Nope." She eyed the tattered piece. "I'm kind of glad, too. Looks a little cumbersome."

"You get used to it." He shrugged. "Here." He placed the helmet on her head. "How does that feel?"

"It's not near as heavy as I would have expected." Since it was too big, she reached a hand to steady it.

He stood back and smiled. "You look awful cute. But then, you always look cute."

The wink that accompanied his comment had a wave of heat creeping into her cheeks. Removing the helmet, she turned so he wouldn't see. Cleared her throat. "That's the sort of thing that would be perfect for the exhibit. That is, if you're okay with it."

"No, I think it's a great idea." He set it back in the box, adding the tissue paper and lid before picking it up. "I'll set it over here with the other items." The adjacent dining room-turned-home gym was the designated drop zone for all potential museum items.

Grace moved over to the box he'd been working on.

Retrieved a stack of photos. "Have you considered loaning them one of your uniforms?"

Now standing at the end of the sofa, hands resting low on his hips, he shook his head. "I can't believe I didn't think of that. I mean, I've got an entire closet full of uniforms."

"Looks like we just came up with another item."

"Which uniform, though?"

Continuing to shuffle through pictures, she said, "If you still have one of your combat uniforms that would be good. Especially since Mama talked about you bringing things into the twenty-first century." She glanced his way, shrugging. "The Universal Camouflage Pattern does just that."

"Okay." He moved beside her, picking up the photos he'd been working on before. "I'll grab it later. Just don't let me forget."

"Are these pictures of you in Afghanistan?" She fanned out three images. One of him in full gear, standing near a Humvee, another of him with a series of tents in the background and yet another of him in the desert.

He leaned closer. Close enough for her to feel the warmth radiating from his bare arms. "Yep. Those were from my second tour."

"I'm sure they could scan these, maybe blow them up to use in the display."

"We can always offer."

"Do you have an envelope or a zip-top bag I could put them in so they won't get lost?"

"Sure. Just give me one second."

While she waited, she continued to sift through the plethora of photos. "You know, at some point, you should consider sorting all these out and putting them in albums."

He reappeared, holding a plastic Baggie. "That sounds about as much fun as watching paint dry."

Without thinking, she elbowed him in the side. "I'm serious." She snatched the bag.

He flinched then rubbed his ribs as though she'd hurt him. "I know you are. Let's just say it's not high on my priority list right now."

She dropped the photos into the bag. "Well, you should at least think about it."

Continuing to look at snapshots, she came across one of Kaleb looking very handsome in his dress uniform with his arms around the waist of a pretty blonde.

"Who's this?" A strange sensation fluttered through her as she showed him the picture.

"That's Gina."

"Your fiancée."

"*Ex*-fiancée." He looked at Grace, a mischievous grin on his face. "Why? Are you jealous?"

She cast him an incredulous look. "No." To be jealous would mean she had feelings for Kaleb. Feelings that went beyond friendship.

So why is your stomach churning?

Besides, she'd never been the jealous type. At least not until she found out her then-husband had a girlfriend.

"I'm just teasing you, Grace."

Two could play at that game. "What would you do if I were jealous?"

"Hmm…" He rubbed his chin, pondering. "Well, first I'd be flattered."

"Pfft." She waved a hand. "Typical male."

"And then—" he moved closer, slipping his arms around her waist "—I'd do everything I could to prove that you had no reason to worry."

Looking into his smoldering eyes, her heart stopped. She could easily believe that any woman fortunate enough to have a man like Kaleb would never have cause for alarm.

But she certainly did. His lips were mere inches from hers. All she had to do was push up onto her tiptoes—

"Easy, soldier." She pressed a hand to his chest. "We have work to do."

He hesitated a moment, his smile as teasing as it was tempting, before finally moving away. "Can I get you something to drink? Diet Dr Pepper, perhaps?"

Considering how warm it had suddenly got— "Since when do you have Diet Dr Pepper?"

He started toward the kitchen. "Since I picked some up at the store the other day."

She eased onto the sofa, her legs feeling a bit wobbly. Not only did he know her favorite drink, he actually made the effort to go out and get it.

"Here you go." He handed her a cold can.

"Thanks." Sinking back into the overstuffed cushions, she surreptitiously watched him as he moved across the hardwood floor and opened another box. *A man who loves through actions, not words.*

"Hey, I forgot all about this." He reached inside the box and pulled out a uniform shirt. But it wasn't like the others. "This came from my Afghan friend Akram." He held up the desert camo shirt. "He was one of our translators. He gave me this in exchange for a pair of Nikes."

"Really?" She scooted to the edge of her seat, but still didn't trust herself to stand.

"He was a pretty cool guy." Kaleb turned the uniform this way and that. "Think they'd like to have this at the museum?"

"They might. I mean, it's definitely not something people see every day." She popped the top on her drink. Took a sip. "Add it to the pile and let them decide."

After setting her soda on the side table, she grabbed

another wad of pictures from the box in front of her. The guy had enough photos to fill a hundred albums.

She shuffled through them. Desert. Desert. Armored vehicle. Hmph. The next image was of Kaleb in full combat uniform, playing soccer with a group of children. She thumbed to the next one. Kaleb sitting with a dog and three little boys, his grin as big as the sun. Another was of him holding a smiling little girl. And yet another of him cradling an infant.

"Whatcha got there?"

She hadn't realized he was beside her. "More pictures." She handed them to him, her heart twisting as a smile bloomed on his face.

"Oh, yeah." His head bobbed up and down as he studied the images. "The kids were great. To see their smiling faces in the midst of such chaos always did wonders for our battle-scarred souls. And they loved to play soccer." His thoughtful gaze drifted from the pictures to her. "It never ceased to amaze me that, even though they were surrounded by death and destruction, they were always ready with a smile."

She reached for her soda can, trying to ignore the ache that leached into her chest. "From what I've heard, kids can be pretty resilient."

He gestured to the photos. "This is living proof."

Though she already knew the answer, she asked anyway. "You really like kids, don't you?"

"Are you kidding? Kids are great." Grinning, he tossed the pictures on the table. "But you'll find that out soon enough, *Aunt Grace*."

As Kaleb returned to the other side of the room, a tempest of unwanted emotions whirled inside her. Somewhere along the way, no matter how hard she'd tried to fight it or told herself they were just friends, she'd foolishly opened her heart to Kaleb. Allowing him to take up residence in those areas she'd deemed off-limits.

Now she'd pay the price.

Thankfully, she was leaving. Because if she were to stay in Ouray, she'd only grow more attached. And seeing the look on his face just now as he spoke about the kids, one thing came through loud and clear.

She could never be the woman for him.

He had to check out that sway bar link. Whenever a rental vehicle was down, it meant a loss of income. Yet Sami insisted she needed his help.

Forgoing his internet search for replacement bolts, he dropped his smartphone on the office counter and looked at the computer screen.

"I've got a customer on hold. I'm trying to deduct their coupon, but the computer won't let me. It keeps showing the original price."

This was so not his forte. Vehicles he knew. Computers, not so much.

He studied the monitor, glancing at the time stamp in the corner, wondering how much longer before Grace would be back. Since Roger was scheduled for a tour, she'd taken her mother to Montrose for a follow-up with the cardiologist.

"Did you click on Apply Coupon?"

Sami sent him a look. "Kaleb, I am not an idiot. Of course I clicked Apply Coupon."

"Okay, okay." He contemplated the issue awhile longer. "You'll just have to tell the people we'll get back to them with their total and then let Grace handle it." Technology. It was great when it worked the way it was supposed to, stank when it didn't. "I'll be in the garage if you need me."

He quickly moved back into the shop, the smells of

rubber and petroleum products doing little to calm him. Even he didn't understand why he was so stressed. After all, his deadline with the museum had been met, business was great and the sway bar could be as simple as tightening a couple of bolts. So why was he wound up tighter than a two-dollar watch?

Easy. Because the families would be arriving next week and he was supposed to be giving some speech about being a hero at the museum ribbon cutting.

Regardless of what Grace had said about God's providence, he still wasn't comfortable being labeled a hero. He'd relived that night in the Humvee over and over in his dreams, both waking and not, and in every one of them, he was laughing and joking with his buddies right before the explosion.

Those were not the actions of a hero.

Continuing under the lift, he stared up into the carriage of the Jeep Wrangler. This he understood. With the help of an impact wrench, he removed the lug nuts and pulled off the front tires to give him a better look at the issue.

Wait a minute. He was going to order some extra replacement bolts to have on hand.

He reached for the phone on his belt, but it wasn't there. Where had…?

He groaned. He'd left his phone inside. However, the last thing he wanted was to get drawn into another one of Sami's computer issues. He shook his head.

The phone could wait.

After successfully tightening one bolt and replacing another, he reattached the wheels and lowered the vehicle. He'd need to take it for a test drive before renting it again. Didn't want customers having any problems. Especially when they could have been avoided in the first place.

He again made his way into the office, praying Sami

wasn't having more computer issues. "Mom, what are you doing here?" He continued toward the desk and gave her a one-armed hug.

She held a finger to her lips. "Shh. Sami's talking to Vanessa."

"Vanessa?" Beau's Vanessa?

He jerked his gaze to his sister, mortified to see that she was using his phone.

"A cookout is an excellent idea. And forget about the park—my parents would be thrilled to have all of you over."

"Cookout? What?"

Sami waved him off like a madwoman. "You are not imposing at all. My mother was just mentioning that we needed to have some sort of get-together that first night, so I guess great minds think alike."

Seemed everyone and his sister was excited about the families' upcoming visit. Everyone except him, that was.

"Aw, I'm looking forward to meeting you, too, Vanessa. See you soon." Sami ended the call.

"What are you doing?" He strode behind the desk and grabbed his phone.

"You left your phone in here. It rang. I saw Vanessa's name and figured I'd answer."

"Yeah, well, you figured wrong."

"Kaleb, that is no way to talk to your sister. She was simply trying to help."

He looked at his mother. "Sorry, Mom, but that was my business to handle, not Sami's."

"What's got you in such a bad mood?" Sami glared at him.

"You." He slammed the phone onto its clip and started for the door. "I've gotta test-drive that Jeep. I'll be back later."

"How much lat—" The slamming door cut Sami off.

He knew he should feel bad, but he was too agitated to care. He was worried enough about coming face-to-face with his friends' family members as it was. Now they were planning some big shindig at his parents'? Without asking him? Out of the question.

But how could he retract the offer now?

He climbed into the bright blue Jeep. Maybe he wouldn't have to show up.

Under a clear blue sky, he headed north out of town, turning off at County Road 14, the road to Lake Lenore and the old Bachelor-Syracuse Mine. Of course, he bypassed both destinations and continued farther up, onto rockier terrain. That should give the vehicle a sufficient workout. It wasn't uncommon for these bumpy mountain roads to sometimes vibrate the bolts loose.

His grip tightened on the steering wheel as he maneuvered onto a tree-lined trail. Why did Grace have to be gone today? She wouldn't have answered his personal phone. Even if she had, she wouldn't have made plans for him. Now he was committed to something he'd never agreed to in the first place.

He needed to talk to Grace. Since handing his stuff over to the museum on Saturday, he hadn't seen her as much. Well, at least not after hours. He couldn't blame her for wanting to spend time with her mother, but he missed the teasing and playful banter. Even the probing conversations.

Yeah, Grace could help him sort through all of this.

Convinced that everything was in perfect working order, he turned around and drove back into town, going straight to Roger and Donna's. Perhaps he could catch Grace before she went back to the office.

He pulled up in front of the house only to discover that no one was home.

Sitting inside the Jeep with the windows rolled down,

he drew in a deep breath and allowed himself to get lost in the mountain views. *Lord, help me.*

At the sound of gravel crunching behind him, he looked in his rearview mirror to see Grace and her mother pulling up in Donna's SUV.

He could feel himself relax a notch as they eased into the drive.

He exited the Jeep and went to assist Donna.

He opened the passenger door and offered his hand. "How did the appointment go?" His own issues paled in comparison to what Donna, Grace and Roger had gone through.

Looking as lovely as ever, Donna took hold and gracefully stepped onto the gravel drive. "He said I was doing great."

Grace exited the driver's side, tossing the door closed behind her. "He also said that she needed to continue to take things easy and come back in two more weeks."

"Ack." Donna waved a hand, looking much like her daughter. "Details."

He laid her hand in the crook of his elbow. "When we're talking about your heart, though, those details can be kind of important."

"Yes, I suppose you're right." She guided him toward the back door. "Would you care to join us for lunch?"

"No, Mama. Kaleb and I have to get back to work. You need to rest. This has been the most activity you've had since you got out of the hospital."

Donna let go a sigh. "Yes, dear."

Once Grace had her mother settled, she shooed Kaleb out the door, following on his heels. "What are you doing here?"

They continued down the back steps and around the side of the house.

"Oh, I blew up at Sami."

"What happened?"

A pair of broad-tailed hummingbirds whizzed past them, aiming for the feeder hanging from Donna's porch.

"Vanessa, the wife of my buddy Beau I told you about? She called."

Hands shoved in the pockets of her denim skirt, Grace squinted against the sun. "What does that have to do with Sami?"

"I made the mistake of leaving my cell phone in the office, so my sister took the liberty of answering it. My mom was there, too. Next thing I know, they're planning to have some big cookout the night the families arrive."

They paused beside the Jeep.

Grace's gaze narrowed. "And the problem with that is what?"

"You know my fears about seeing the families. And just thinking about that speech they want me to give at the ribbon cutting has me so stressed out I'm likely to snap at any moment. Which is pretty much what I did with Sami." He scraped his boot across the gravel, shrugged. "You always seem to know how to cut to the chase and help me sort things out. How am I going to do this?"

Crossing her arms over her chest, Grace eyed the leaves on the trees, the neighbor's dog in the yard next door and the grass before turning her focus back to him. "You want to know what you should do."

"Please."

She took a step closer. "Get over yourself." She jammed a finger into his chest. "Those families have spent five years dealing with their own stuff and all you can think about is you. Well, guess what, Kaleb? It's not all about you."

Chapter Fourteen

Grace sat on Mama and Roger's front porch Saturday evening, knees clutched to her chest, her heart heavy. She couldn't go on like this. But what choice did she have?

Memories of her conversation with Kaleb Thursday afternoon had plagued her brain. Even now, they made her cringe.

After realizing just how strong her feelings had grown for him, she'd purposely worked to put some distance between them. Completing the task for the museum definitely made that easier. But after a rough morning with Mama, dealing with her fears of life never being the same, Grace snapped, sounding absolutely horrid, even to her own ears.

Wearing the most comfy pair of shorts she could find, she stretched her legs out on the white wicker love seat. The evening air was still, the temperature hovering somewhere around perfect. The sun had dropped behind Ouray's western slope, though there was still plenty of daylight. Maybe, if she kept watching, there'd be an alpenglow.

She felt bad that she hadn't apologized to Kaleb for her behavior. But it was probably for the best. That was, if she truly wanted to keep her distance.

Which she did. Most of the time. Deep inside, though,

she missed him. Missed the way he took such pleasure in the simple things, like campfires and Cascade Falls. The way he seemed to know just what she needed exactly when she needed it. Most of all, she missed the comfort of his embrace and how he made her feel special. Wanted.

The sound of shifting gravel stirred her from her musing.

Peering over the side of the porch, she spotted a jogger. Every muscle in her body tensed.

Basketball shorts, a sweaty tank top and a prosthetic. Kaleb.

She tried to disappear into the brightly colored floral cushions of the love seat, but it was too late.

Still a house away, he came to a complete stop. His eyes riveted to her. Hands on his hips, he watched her for what seemed like an eternity. His scrutiny was unnerving to say the least, but, try as she might, she couldn't make herself move to go inside.

Finally, he started again.

She released the breath she'd been holding, closing her eyes for a moment.

"You okay?"

Her eyes flew wide.

Kaleb was standing at the bottom of the steps.

She straightened in her seat, swinging her bare feet over the side. "Fine. Yeah." She tucked her hair behind her ear. "I'm good."

"Glad to hear it." Using the handrail for support, he climbed the wooden steps and continued toward her, the blade he used for running making a gentle thump against the white floorboards.

While her pulse set off for parts unknown, a plethora of monarchs took flight in her midsection.

"Mind if I sit?" He gestured to one of the wicker chairs.

"No. Go ahead." She grabbed the throw pillow from behind her and clutched it in front of her. "Out for your nightly run?"

Sitting, he rested his elbows on his thighs, clasped his hands together and looked her square in the eye. "Yes, but I also wanted to see you. I owe you an apology, Grace."

Seriously? Hadn't they been through this before? Obviously he was much better at apologizing than she'd ever be. And while the first time he apologized had been justified, this time, she wasn't so sure.

"I thought about what you said and realize I came on a little strong the other day, forcing my problems onto you. I had no right to do that."

No right? Weren't they supposed to be friends? Of course, he had a right to expect his friend to listen. That was the kind of thing friends did.

Except she shut him down.

So what was she going to do now?

"I thought that voice sounded far too deep for Grace." Roger pushed through the screen door. "I didn't know you guys had plans tonight." His gaze moved between her and Kaleb.

"We don't." Kaleb ran a hand through his sweat-dampened hair. "I was just out for my run and thought I'd stop and say hi."

Always the gentleman. Making her feel like an even bigger jerk.

"Nice night, that's for sure." Hands buried in the pockets of his cargo shorts, Roger looked out over the neighborhood. "Probably one of the best ones we've had so far this year."

She glanced at Kaleb. Caught him watching her.

She quickly looked away, heat creeping into her cheeks as she pretended to be enthralled in the colorful flower basket hanging overhead.

"It has been an interesting year." Though she refused to look, she knew Kaleb's eyes hadn't left her.

"Roger?" Mama pushed the door open. "Why, hello, Kaleb." A smile lit her face. Even though it had been only two days since they went to the doctor, she seemed to be feeling a lot better, which, in turn, had improved her outlook on everything else.

Kaleb stood and went to greet her. "We were just enjoying this perfect weather. Care to join us?" He motioned to the chair he'd vacated.

"It is lovely out here, isn't it?" Mama breathed deep, gazing out over the yard as though seeing it for the first time. "I do believe I've been cooped up in that house for too long."

Roger took hold of her arm. "Come on. Let's sit." He escorted her to the chair closest to the love seat before taking the seat beside her.

"Have a seat, Kaleb, so we can discuss the exhibit."

A look of panic flitted across his handsome, though sweaty, features. Considering the only seat available was on the love seat, next to Grace...

She scooted over, getting as close to the arm as possible before patting the cushion beside her. "I promise not to bite."

Mama leaned back in her chair and addressed Kaleb. "I spoke with Delores Whitley today. She is absolutely thrilled with your donations and says the exhibit is coming together even better than they'd hoped."

Kaleb was on the edge of his seat, as though ready to flee at any moment. "Good. Though I can't take much credit. It's Grace we have to thank. Without her, I'm afraid I wouldn't have been much help at all."

Grace's gaze slid sideways. *Oh, just rake the knife of guilt over my heart, why don't you.*

"I know what you mean." Mama reached for her hand. Gave it a quick squeeze. "Without her, I might not even be here."

How many times had she heard that since moving in. "Mama…"

The woman leaned back again. "So, how's your speech for the ribbon cutting coming along? It's only a week away."

If it was possible, even more sweat beaded Kaleb's brow. "I'm still mulling over what I want to say."

Grace dared to face him this time. Mulling, her eye. If anything, he was trying to figure out how to get out of it.

"Really? Well, I wouldn't take too long. It'll be here before you know it and you want to be prepared."

No doubt about it, Mama was definitely feeling more like her old self.

"Yes, ma'am."

Grace actually felt sorry for Kaleb. Poor guy came to apologize and ended up being grilled.

"Oh, goodness." Mama covered a yawn with her hand. "I guess all of this fresh air is getting to me." Gripping the arms of her chair, she pushed to her feet. "I should think about getting to bed."

Roger was already standing, offering his arm. "I'm right behind you, dear."

They turned for the door.

Mama waved. "You kids have a good night."

"Good night," they said in unison.

As Roger and Mama disappeared into the house, Grace wrestled with how to respond to Kaleb's apology. If she coldly accepted it then they'd carry on, with every interaction being as awkward as they'd been these past few days. Or she could apologize to him and enjoy one of the greatest friendships she'd ever had. But doing that also meant putting her heart on the line. Was that something she was willing to risk?

Kaleb stood. "I should—"

"Wait." Tossing the pillow aside, she jumped to her feet. "You don't owe me anything, Kaleb, least of all an apology. I was having a bad day Thursday and I took it out on you."

"Yeah, but I shouldn't have—"

She held up a hand to cut him off. "We've shared a lot over these last several weeks. Of course, you would have expected you could vent without fear of having your head bit off. But I did just that. And I had no right. So I apologize."

Hands on his hips, he stared at the painted floor. "Here's the problem, though."

Her heart sank. She'd blown it. Kaleb was one of the sweetest, most genuine people she'd ever known and she'd stomped all over his feelings.

He looked at her now. "You were right. It's not all about me. Yet I keep trying to make it that way."

As daylight faded and night sounds filled the air, she breathed a sigh of relief and smiled up at her friend. "I don't have a campfire, but if you'd care to sit and talk, perhaps we could figure out that speech of yours."

The corners of his mouth lifted. "That'd be great." He hesitated a few seconds. Scratched his head. "Okay, this might be pushing it, but how would you feel about accompanying me to a cookout Thursday? Strictly for moral support."

She knew how anxious he was about seeing his friends' families. Though she believed his worry unfounded. Still, they were very real to him and she wanted to help.

"What's on the menu?"

"Meat."

She couldn't help grinning. "Then it looks like you've got yourself a date, my friend."

Any other time, Kaleb would have been over the moon to be in the company of such a gorgeous woman. Yet while Grace was beyond stunning in a long turquoise sundress and strappy sandals, he simply wanted to make it through tonight.

"Kaleb?"

They paused in the street.

She took hold of his hands and stared deeply into his eyes. "I'm here for you." She gently squeezed. "It's going to be fine. I promise."

He appreciated her reassurance, though it did little to bolster him. Still, he was beyond grateful to have her with him. Since that night on Roger and Donna's porch, they'd spent a lot of time together, both at work and after hours. And while they hadn't acknowledged their feelings, it was as though they'd both accepted them, becoming comfortable with the occasional touch or embrace. Though he had yet to kiss her again.

"Are you ready?"

Standing in front of his parents' two-story folk-style home, he blew out a breath. One. Two. *Lord, please give me the words to say to these people. And don't let them hate me.*

With one hand in Grace's and the other tucked inside the pocket of his khaki cargo shorts, he said, "Okay. Let's go."

The aroma of grilled meat filled the air as they moved across the lush green yard, aiming for the oversized wooden deck on the home's south side.

"Here they are now." His mother, Bev, strolled across the deck, meeting them at the steps. She and Grace must have compared notes, because she also wore a long sundress, her chin-length blond hair pulled up in a clip.

"Sorry we're late." Addressing the large group of people that milled about, he tamped down his panic and forced a smile. "Had to finish up some things at the shop."

Vanessa approached him, her sable hair pulled back into a ponytail, her dark eyes swimming with tears. "It's so good to see you again." Her hug was fierce, full of warmth and welcome.

When they finally released, a young girl came near him. She was beautiful, looking so much like Beau with her blond curls, carrying a small bouquet of flowers. "These are for you, Mr. Kaleb." She curtsied as though he were some kind of royalty.

Overcome with emotion, he dropped to his knee and hugged the child for all he was worth. Beau would be so proud of his daughter.

As he stood, a man came closer, stopping beside Vanessa.

"This is my fiancé, Brandon," she said.

The dark-haired man, somewhere close to Kaleb's age, extended his hand. "It's an honor. I've heard a lot about you."

Vanessa grabbed hold of Brandon's arm. "We're getting married next week."

Married? How could that be? Had she forgotten about Beau?

Before he had time to think further, another woman moved toward him. "I'm Shannon White. Jason Meador was my husband." Tears spilled onto her round cheeks as she motioned another man forward.

"Ron White." He shook Kaleb's hand. "It's good to finally meet you."

Kaleb's throat thickened. Vanessa was about to get married. Jason's wife had already remarried.

He felt a hand on his shoulder. Turning, he saw Grace smiling.

She leaned toward him. "Remember, it's been five long years for them."

He simply stared at her, understanding dawning. "Thanks for the reminder." Because in many ways, it seemed like only yesterday.

How did she know what he was thinking?

A slightly older man and woman made their way to him.

The man reached out his hand. "Ron and Michelle Squires, Stephen's parents." The man's voice broke.

Before Kaleb could respond, the man pulled him close, sobbing.

Tears welled in Kaleb's eyes. He'd been ready for them to hate him, but he hadn't counted on this.

When the Squires finally retreated, another couple moved closer.

Again, the man held out his hand. "Kurt and Abigail Kowalski. Dayton's folks."

Kaleb couldn't contain himself any longer. Dayton had been the youngest among them. Barely making it to his twentieth birthday. Gulping for air, he hugged the couple. His body shook as he gave in to his emotions, not only with grief for what these people had lost, but for the love they'd shown him.

When the Kowalskis had also retreated, Kaleb was beside himself. Overwhelmed and shocked beyond words. He'd come in here on the defensive and found himself surrounded by people who genuinely cared.

He felt an arm around his shoulders.

Without even looking, he knew it was Grace.

She handed him a napkin. "I think I speak for Kaleb and the rest of his family when I say that we are blessed to have each and every one of you here. We look forward to hearing your stories, so, please, enjoy yourselves."

He dried his eyes, watching her step aside.

Grace was exactly what he'd been looking for when he began his search for an office manager. Someone who could easily handle those things that didn't come naturally to him. Someone who shared his vision and whose skill set complemented his own. In Grace, he'd found the perfect partner. Except tonight, those thoughts had nothing to do with business.

Where he was weak, she was strong. She wasn't afraid to step in and lift him up. He only prayed he could do the same for her.

"Is everybody ready to eat?" His father, Tom, stood beside the grill, spatula raised in the air.

His query was met with a resounding "Yes!"

"All right, then. If everyone would join hands, I'd like to offer a blessing."

Everyone did as he'd requested, quickly forming a crude circle.

Kaleb took hold of Grace's hand, giving it a gentle squeeze of thanks.

She glanced at him and smiled.

"If you'd bow your heads, please." Dad began. "Father God, we thank You for this day and for these people who've traveled far to be with us. I ask a special blessing on each and every one of them. Lord, we ask that You would bless this food to the nourishment of our bodies, in Jesus's name, amen."

"Amen."

Sometime later, after he'd relaxed enough to allow himself to grab a burger, he stood at the edge of the deck, watching Beau's daughter, Hannah, and Vanessa's fiancé playing soccer in the yard. It still broke his heart that his friend had never got the chance to meet his little girl. That she'd had to grow up without her father.

He looked intently at Vanessa's fiancé, Brandon. Did he always play with Hannah or was this interaction just for show?

"He's a good man."

Kaleb startled at Vanessa's voice. Had she really known what he was thinking?

"He seems okay."

"We met when Hannah was three." Arms folded across her chest, she watched her daughter and fiancé. "It's taken me a long time to find someone who could hold a candle to Beau." She smiled. "But I finally found him."

Spotting them, Brandon waved and jogged toward them. "I can't believe this place. There are mountains everywhere I look."

Kaleb couldn't help but grin, eyeing the peaks around them. "Yeah, nestled in a bowl like this makes Ouray pretty special."

"When Vanessa told me where we were going, I had no idea. But this is incredible."

Hannah trotted toward them then. "Daddy, come on." She motioned for Brandon to join her.

"Sorry. Duty calls." Brandon hurried off.

Kaleb's heart skidded to a stop. Daddy? That was a title that should have been reserved for Beau.

But you wanted Hannah to have a father.

"Brandon is planning to adopt Hannah."

He faced Vanessa. "I think Beau would approve."

Her eyes welled with tears. "I think so, too."

"Kaleb."

He turned to see the Kowalskis headed toward him. Vanessa touched his arm. "I'll catch up with you later."

She made her way down the steps to join Brandon and Hannah.

"Hope you all are enjoying yourselves." He leaned against the deck rail.

"Beautiful town you have here." Kurt lifted his gaze.

"Wait until we take you on one of our tours. You'll get to see a whole lot more."

Abigail seemed to bubble with excitement. "I can't wait."

Kurt's expression turned more somber then. "Our Dayton thought very highly of you."

Kaleb swallowed hard. "He was a good kid. A fine soldier. I was proud to know him."

"He admired you a great deal," said Abigail. "Used to talk about you all the time."

Kurt pulled a paper from his shirt pocket. "He sent this email shortly before he died. We thought you might like to have it." He handed it to Kaleb.

He opened the paper, noting that one section had been highlighted.

I can't say where, but we were in a firefight the other day. And out in the middle was this woman and her kid. Next thing I know, Sgt. Palmer yells for us to cover him. Crazy fool ran right into the cross fire, grabbed the kid and shielded the woman until they were safely behind us. Talk about selfless. That's the kind of hero I hope I can be.

"Wow." It was all he could manage.

"You were a good example for those young men out there." Kurt sniffed. "You should be proud."

"Thank you, sir."

As the Kowalskis walked away, Grace moved alongside him. "Tough night in some ways, uplifting in others."

"You got that right." He reached for her hand. "And I realized something."

"What's that?"

He scanned the faces that had traveled to be with him. "They've all moved on." He looked at Grace now. "The past is a part of them, but it doesn't define them."

She laid a hand against his chest. "Perhaps we could both learn from that."

Chapter Fifteen

The sun was shining brightly when Kaleb and Grace arrived at the museum early Saturday afternoon. Flags swayed in the breeze, as did the red-white-and-blue banner over the museum door that read Welcome to Our Hometown Heroes.

People had already begun to gather. He recognized many of them as townspeople; however, there were just as many folks that he didn't recognize.

"There's my handsome son." His mom emerged from the small crowd, phone in hand, dodging a couple of people in the process.

"You're looking pretty good yourself, Mom." Her favorite white dress was accented by a pair of glitzy sandals.

As usual, Dad brought up the rear. "Son." He held out his hand. When Kaleb took hold, his father reeled him in for a hug. "I'm proud of you."

Even though it wasn't the first time he'd heard those words from his father, his throat still thickened.

"Get in the shade so I can take your picture." His mother pointed to a grassy spot.

Grace let go of his arm and stepped away.

"No, no, Grace." Mom waved her back toward him. "I want you in the picture."

Considering she was wearing a dress for the second time this week, he wanted her in it, too.

He slid his arm around her waist, inhaling the sweet floral fragrance he'd come to recognize as uniquely her. He liked having her with him. If only he could convince her that Ouray was where she belonged. With her family. With him.

Likewise, Grace slipped her arm around him. "I'm glad my mom suggested you wear your uniform." She smiled up at him. "You make that thing look good, soldier."

The comment sent a strange sensation whirling inside him. One that had nothing to do with his speech.

"Smile." Mom held up her phone. A second later, she stared at the screen. "Cute couple."

"Let me see." Coming from behind them, Donna slowly sidled up to his mom and studied the shot. "Aww... You'll have to send that one to me."

He pulled Grace against him. "Hear that? We make a cute couple."

"Yeah, I heard." A blush crept into her cheeks as she eased out of his grip.

"Sorry, but I need to borrow Kaleb for a minute." Donna took him by the arm and led him along the front of the stone building that had once been a hospital. A podium adorned with red-white-and-blue bunting had been positioned to the right of the main entrance.

"We'll have all of our donors lined up along here." She gestured to the sidewalk. "You're welcome to hold the microphone or leave it on the podium, whatever you're comfortable with. By the way, you're going to be the last one to speak."

Yes, let's just prolong the agony.

"Where's Roger?"

"Right here."

Kaleb turned to see his friend sporting a blue garrison cap with the VFW emblem. He choked back a laugh. "Nice hat."

Roger smirked. "Hey, I'm not the one wearing a beret."

Beyond his friend, he saw Grace talking with Vanessa and the other families. "Excuse me, please."

He wove his way toward the group. Seeing them no longer filled him with dread. Instead, they gave him hope for the future.

Yesterday, he'd taken everyone on a Jeep tour over Imogene Pass. What a great group of people. They had so much fun. There had even been talk of making this reunion an annual event. Maybe next time he'd suggest they come for an old-fashioned Ouray Fourth of July.

"Afternoon, everyone."

"Afternoon!" They responded in unison.

"If you wouldn't mind, I'd like to get a group picture with all of you." He handed Grace his phone. "Do you mind?"

"Of course not. Why don't you all get up on the steps there so we can get everyone in the shot."

They huddled together, Kaleb in the middle at the bottom.

"Cheese."

A few minutes later, Roger tapped him on the shoulder. "They're ready for us."

"Okay." He turned to Grace.

"You'll do fine." She ran a hand along the breast of his jacket.

"As long as I know you're here."

She smiled. "So what are you waiting for?"

Kaleb lined up to the side of the podium with the five other men. He knew Phil Purcell, the father of his friend Gage, who'd served in the Marines, and Clay Musgrove, caretaker of the Bachelor-Syracuse Mine, who, like Roger, had served in Vietnam. The other two, one a Korean War vet, the other Desert Storm, Kaleb wasn't familiar with.

Delores Whitley, the museum's director, took the podium to welcome everyone. "Today, we are here to honor our hometown heroes. Those who have served our country, never to be forgotten." She briefly explained what the exhibit was about and what folks might find there.

The Korean War vet was the first to speak, followed by Roger, Clay, Phil and the Desert Storm guy. Some shared stories, while others spoke about what it meant to them to serve their country.

Finally, it was Kaleb's turn. He set his notes on the podium, electing to leave the microphone right where it was. Then he stared out at the hundred or so faces before him, scanning them until he found Vanessa, Shannon White, the Squires and the Kowalskis.

Suddenly, he had the clarity he had been hoping for all along. He knew exactly what he was supposed to say. And it came from the heart.

He shoved his notes aside. "The theme for this exhibit is hometown heroes. However, not one of us standing up here today is a hero. We're just ordinary people who were put in extraordinary circumstances and forced to step out of our comfort zones."

He cleared his throat. "As some of you may know, while serving in the Middle East, I was injured by an IED. But the four men with me that day perished. They paid the ultimate price for our freedom. They are the true heroes."

Applause filled the air. Only this time, he didn't mind it so much. Because it wasn't for him. It was for those who rightfully deserved it.

When the noise wound down, he continued. "Thank you for coming today. And I hope you enjoy the exhibit."

Stepping away from the podium, he sought out Grace.

Just the sight of her made him smile. No matter what she said or did, his heart refused to be derailed.

She was clapping along with everyone else, but the wink she sent was just for him and he knew he'd made her proud.

In that moment, he knew he couldn't let her go. And before this day was out, he had to tell her how he felt.

While cake was served to those in attendance, Kaleb and the other five donors, along with a photographer from the local newspaper, were led inside the museum for the official ribbon cutting at the room holding the display.

Later, he and Grace and the families made their way inside.

Looking at everything from photos to uniforms to World War I weaponry, he had to admit that he was impressed. They'd managed to span every era from World War I to today.

"There's my daddy!" Hannah pointed to a photo of Beau, Jason, Stephen, Dayton and Kaleb standing in front of their Humvee.

He turned to Grace. "Was that in my stuff?"

She nodded. "We had it blown up for the exhibit. Along with a few extra copies. There's an eight-by-ten for each of you."

While the families enjoyed the entire museum, Kaleb whisked Grace outside and, with Donna's permission, into the log cabin that sat to the side of the main building.

"What are you doing?"

Envisioning a future with Grace had become second nature. The way they seemed to work toward the common goal of building a successful business reminded him of his parents.

He'd never forget the day they opened the Palmer Realty office. Seeing their dedication to each other, their family, as well as their business. He wanted that. A partner. A helpmate.

Grace was all of that. And so much more. She understood things he couldn't even put into words.

"This." Slipping an arm around her waist, he pulled her to him and kissed her.

Her arms wound around his neck, filling him with hope.

When the kiss ended, he watched her, waiting to see if she had any regrets.

Instead, she gave him a shy smile. "What took you so long?"

He laughed, tucking her head under his chin as he held her close. He caressed her silky hair, noting how perfectly they fit together. As though they were made for each other.

When she lifted her head, he combed his fingers through her hair. "I don't want you to leave, Grace. I love you. Please, stay in Ouray."

Her stunned eyes searched his. "Y-you love me?"

"With all of my heart." Then he lowered his head and claimed her lips in a kiss that would erase any doubt. Grace was his future. And even though she was supposed to leave, he was trusting God to work out the details. Because living without her was not an option.

Grace was on the front porch Sunday evening, putting on a pair of strappy sandals, when she saw Kaleb walk up. He was wearing shorts again. Denim this time, along with a deep maroon polo shirt that hugged those massive biceps.

She liked a man who was comfortable in his own skin.

The families had left today, promising to extend their visit next time. She'd really enjoyed her time with them. It was because of them that Kaleb had grown. Learning to accept the past and move forward.

"Wow!" Kaleb's appreciative smile when he spotted her set her insides to bubbling. She felt as though she were at a junior high school dance. And just as petrified.

She had yet to respond to his declaration of love or his request that she stay in Ouray. Interestingly enough, she'd received an email from the cruise line just this morning, saying that, due to unforeseeable circumstances, the ship's renovations would be delayed and that they would not be able to set sail until November. Making her contract null and void, unless she was to sign an amendment.

"I'm glad you approve." At the last second, she'd chosen to wear the turquoise tank she'd accidentally bought in Montrose the day Mama fell ill, along with a pair of white shorts.

"Grace, you'd look great no matter what you wore."

Her cheeks warmed, though it had nothing to do with the heat. "I think we'd better go."

Sami had invited the family for dinner tonight and she didn't want to be late.

As she descended the steps, Kaleb offered his arm. With him, chivalry was not dead. Things with Kaleb were easy. Comfortable. She still found it hard to believe that he actually loved her.

But did she love him?

She could easily see herself loving him. But fear was a powerful emotion. What if he stopped loving her like Aaron had?

Gravel crunched beneath their feet as they meandered from one street to the next, talking about the weekend's events. The slightest hint of a breeze stirred the evening air as two broad-tailed hummingbirds zipped past them. Their playful cricket-like chirps still amazed her, since every hummingbird she'd ever seen was silent.

He stopped and kissed her. Every nerve ending in her body went on high alert. Kaleb made her feel cherished. And more alive than she had in a very long time.

Resting her head against his chest, she sighed and listened to the pounding of his heart. She savored the strength of his embrace and the protection it offered. He was the kind of man she had always dreamed of. Was it possible that her dreams had finally come true? Was there really a hope and a future for them?

They started walking again, stopping a few blocks later.

"And here we are." Kaleb paused in front of a cute single-story house that she suspected was new construction, yet had the charm of an older home. "You smell that, Grace?"

She sniffed the air. "Meat." On the grill, of course. Smiling, she closed her eyes and inhaled deeper. "Ribs… Chicken… Burgers…" Opening her eyes, she glanced up at Kaleb. "Smells like the three basic food groups to me."

His grin was priceless. "You're my kind of woman."

That comment, coupled with the protective feel of his hand against the small of her back as he urged her up the walkway, robbed her of all rational thought. And had her wondering if, just maybe, she really could entrust her heart to someone again.

Holding her hand, Kaleb rang the bell.

Sami swung open the door. "About time you two got here."

"Hey, it's not like we have a business to run or anything." Kaleb pushed past his sister, bringing Grace with him.

Grace couldn't help noticing how he used the plural sense. As if Mountain View Tours belonged to both of them.

Jack charged toward Kaleb. "I'm a monster twuck."

Kaleb intercepted him, flipping him end over end until he rested on Kaleb's shoulder. "You're a monster all right."

Jack giggled when Kaleb tickled his belly.

While Kaleb set Jack on the floor, Sami gave Grace a quick hug before leading them to the back of the house, where Scott was grilling on the patio.

Tom and Bev relaxed in the glider, though Bev quickly stood.

Grace liked her. Liked all of Kaleb's family, for that matter.

Jack charged ahead of them.

"Sorry we're late." Grace continued toward Bev, who was awaiting a hug.

"Uncle Kaleb, I got bubbles." As if to emphasize his claim, Jack dipped the wand into the small red bottle of liquid he held in his other hand, pressed it against his lips and blew. Naturally, the bubble burst without ever making it into the air.

Kaleb crouched to his nephew's level. "Don't touch it to your mouth, soldier. You gotta hold it in front of your mouth, then blow."

Jack dipped the wand again and blew. This time a stream of bubbles took flight, swirling around them. "Yay! I did it."

"You sure did." Kaleb ruffled the boy's curly brown hair, his smile filled with pride.

"Grace, what can I get you to drink?" Sami stood at a table near the French doors that led into the house. "Water? Lemonade? Soda?"

"You don't even have to ask, sister dear," said Kaleb. "Just hand her a Diet Dr Pepper and move on down the road."

"Oh, so I'm that predictable, am I?" Her fist planted firmly on her hip, Grace only pretended to glare at him. "I was actually thinking some lemonade might be nice." She winked at Sami.

A short time later, Sami handed both Grace and Kaleb their drinks. "Now that everyone's here, there's something Scott and I would like to share with all of you."

Tom moved into the circle as Scott slipped an arm around his wife's waist.

Sami peered lovingly up at her husband before addressing everyone else. "We're going to have another baby."

A collective gasp filled the air, followed by a round of cheers.

Bev let go a squeal as she hugged her daughter. "When?"

"January."

Kaleb nabbed his nephew and threw him in the air. "You hear that, Jack? You're going to be a big brother. Just like me."

Tom shook Scott's hand before embracing his daughter. "'Bout time. Your mother's been chomping at the bit for another little one."

"Oh, I have not." Bev dabbed her eyes.

"Congratulations to both of you." While Grace's wishes were sincere, she was helpless to stop the sadness that leached into her heart. What she wouldn't give to be able to make an announcement like that. To be surrounded by excited family members and have a loving husband by her side.

But if past experience was any indication, Grace would likely never experience that same pleasure.

Perhaps God simply didn't want you to have children with Aaron.

Her gaze drifted to Kaleb. With Jack perched on his shoulder, he hugged Sami, his smile explosive. How much greater would his reaction be if the child were his own?

Suddenly chilled, she rubbed at her arms. Kaleb longed for a family. He deserved a family. But, with her, he might never have that joy.

What had she been thinking? She'd allowed herself to get caught up in emotions and had begun to think that, maybe, someone could love her, regardless. That maybe Kaleb was that guy.

Watching the ongoing celebration, she wished she could escape. But she wasn't about to ruin everyone else's good time. She'd put on a happy face and, somehow, make it through the night.

When she and Kaleb finally left, he wrapped his arm around her. "I'm sorry you had to endure that. I could tell you were struggling."

She lifted her face to look at him, trying to pretend all was right in her world. "And why would I be struggling?"

"Because of Sami's announcement." He held her close. "The light in your eyes fades when you're hurting."

"Oh." Could he really read her that well? She drew in a deep breath. "So apparently there's something in the water and everyone's getting pregnant. Your sister, my sister… I'm happy for them."

He tugged her closer. "I know you are. Just remember, you get to be the cool aunt."

She appreciated his attempts to make her feel better. But she cared about him too much to allow him to settle for a what-if.

She'd already decided it would be better for everyone if she just left Ouray. Away from the close-knit community that made her want to call it home. Away from the man who stirred her heart like no one before. And away from the dreams that had dared to take root.

Chapter Sixteen

What a weekend.

Kaleb's time with the families had surpassed all of his expectations. So much so that even an out-of-commission Jeep couldn't bring him down on this rainy, gloomy Monday.

In the span of just a few short days, his outlook on life had done a complete one-eighty. Instead of regret holding him captive to the past, he was now free to contemplate the future. A future he prayed would include Grace.

Since his guides had yet to arrive, the shop was quiet. Kaleb liked it that way. Liked hearing the sound of rain on the tin roof.

Standing beneath the rental Jeep in question, he stared up at a leaky rear differential. Likely the result of being dragged across a rock. It shouldn't take too long to fix. However, due to the weather, it wasn't as if his rentals would be in high demand.

He seated a drain pan to catch the fluid, then grabbed a socket wrench from the rolling tool chest beside him. Telling Grace he loved her had been the right thing to do. Everything was finally out in the open, erasing any doubts she might have had regarding his feelings for her. Now they could concentrate on their future.

He chuckled to himself. The word still seemed foreign to him. Suddenly the future wasn't just about him or his business. Grace was his future. And while they hadn't discussed marriage, it was only logical that that would be the next step. When the time was right, that was. Spring, perhaps. Before the high season set in, limiting their time.

Okay, so maybe he was getting ahead of himself. Because even though he'd told Grace he loved her, she had yet to say she loved him. There was also that issue of her contract with the cruise line.

He removed the first bolt, each turn of the socket wrench making a zip, zip, zip sound. Last night at Sami's, Kaleb couldn't help noticing how well Grace fit in with his family. Grace and his sister had chatted half the night, Sami picking Grace's brain about the places she'd been, while Jack practically wore him out playing ball.

If only his sister's announcement hadn't affected Grace so negatively. He didn't like to see her hurting. He understood her desire to have children and that her ex-husband had done her wrong. However, he wasn't her ex-husband and was determined to do whatever it took to earn her trust.

"Yo, Kaleb."

Glancing over his shoulder, he saw Roger wandering into the garage.

His friend paused beside the tool chest. "Grace said to tell you she was running late. Said she'd be in around nine."

That was odd. Grace was never late. "Is she feeling bad?"

"This is just a guess, but I don't think she got much sleep last night."

"Hmm…" Kaleb couldn't help wondering if it had something to do with the previous evening.

"Problem?" Roger nodded in the direction of the vehicle on the lift.

"Rear dif."

"Fun." He took a step closer to inspect the damage. "So what did you think about Saturday?"

"For all my reservations, I thought it was great."

Roger looked at him now. "Your speech brought the house down."

"Better than having a hundred deadpan faces staring at you."

"You mean like they did with me and the other fellas?"

They both laughed.

Stepping out from beneath the vehicle, Roger continued. "Donna mentioned something about you sneaking Grace out to the log cabin." He toed at something on the concrete. "You two sure have been spending a lot of time together lately."

"You're not going to give me some fatherly warning about your daughter, are you?"

"No. You've sure got Donna's hopes up, though. She likes having Grace here."

Realizing he'd need to open up the office, Kaleb followed his friend. "I know their relationship was a bit strained when Grace first arrived. I'm glad they're doing better." He set his wrench atop the tool chest and picked up a rag.

"Me, too."

"Hey, I pulled your tour truck in." He pointed to the far bay.

"Thanks. Guess I'd better get it dried off and put on the canopy."

"Yeah, and I'd better get inside and unlock the door."

Kaleb stopped at the sink to wash his hands before making his way into the office. He hoped Grace wasn't still bothered about Sami and was half tempted to give her a call and see how she was doing. Then again, if she was trying to get ready for work, he'd just be interrupting. He'd simply have to shove his impatience aside and wait until she got here.

Fortunately, Grace was very thorough, so the clipboards for this morning's tours were already laid out on the counter. Two to Yankee Boy Basin, one to Imogene Pass and the other to Corkscrew. And even though it was raining, the tours would go on.

Once the tours had departed, Kaleb returned to the shop, eager to knock out that differential. Before he even got started, though, the telephone rang, echoing throughout the garage.

Changing directions, he made his way to the tool bench.

"Mountain View Tours, this is Kaleb." He fielded questions from a potential customer and was still on the call when he heard the office door open.

Glancing across the garage, he motioned to Grace. After a slight hesitation, she slowly continued in his direction, looking much the way she had the day she first arrived at Mountain View Tours. Hands tucked in the pockets of her riding jacket, there seemed to be an air of uneasiness about her. But why? Maybe she wasn't feeling well.

"Yes, all of our tours are listed on our website. However, if you have any questions, don't hesitate to give us a call." Ending the call, he met Grace halfway. "Good morning."

He hugged her, though it was kind of like hugging a pole.

When he stepped back, he saw her looking everywhere but at him. Meaning she was uncomfortable about something.

"Grace?" He tilted her chin to look at him. "What's going on?"

Pulling her hand from her pocket, she held out a piece of paper.

"What's this?" Anxiety settled in his gut as he unfolded what looked like a letter and started to read. "You're resigning?" He kept reading, his breaths coming quicker with each word. "Effective immediately?" He looked at her now, his blood roaring in his ears. "Is this supposed to be some kind of joke?" He motioned to the paper.

She lifted her chin. "It's not a joke."

"I don't get it, then. Why would you resign?"

Squaring her shoulders, she said, "Because I'm leaving."

"Leaving? But—I thought we had this all figured out." Panic roiled within him. This couldn't be happening. He couldn't lose her. Not now. Not ever.

"I've been talking with the cruise line. Seems there's been a change in plans."

"I don't believe you." Confusion muddled his brain as he sifted through every conversation they'd had in recent days, looking for any hint that she was considering leaving early. But all he could think about was the way she'd kissed him. No hesitation. No fear. No—

Wait a minute.

"It's because I told you I love you, isn't it? I'm a big boy, Grace. If you don't love me, just tell me." Noting the way she refused to look at him, he stepped closer. "But I don't think that's it. I think you're afraid."

She assumed her toughest stance. "What would I have to be afraid of?"

"Of being hurt again. And your instincts are telling you to run, aren't they?"

"You don't know what you're talking about." She turned to walk away, but he stopped her, turning her to face him.

"Oh, yes, I do. And I've got news for you, Grace. You can run, but you can't hide. Love has a way of taking up residence in your heart, even when you don't want it to. I know that you love me, Grace. You can try to deny it all you want, but I know the truth."

"How could you possibly know what I'm feeling?"

"I lost my leg, but I'm not blind." He stopped, the bitter taste of bile burning the back of his throat as memories of Gina surfaced. "Or is that the problem? That I'm not whole?"

"No!" The word echoed off the concrete floor and walls. "It's because I'm not."

Confusion riddled his mind. "What?"

"I can't have children, Kaleb. You know that."

"So?"

"So, I've seen you with Jack. The smile on your face as you played with him last night. Someday you're going to want kids. You deserve kids." The unshed tears glistening in her eyes made him want to pull her into his arms and will her to believe him. Sure, he'd always dreamed of having his own kids. But more than that, he wanted a life with Grace. With or without kids.

"Then we'll adopt."

Her lip curled. Nostrils flared. "Aaron said the same thing. And we both know how that turned out."

The words hit him like a stun gun. And before he had sense enough to respond, she was gone.

Should-haves and what-ifs pelted his brain. His heart felt as if it might explode. Frustration pulsed through his veins.

Turning, he crumpled the paper in his fist and slammed

it into the red tool chest with a guttural roar even he didn't recognize.

The chest toppled with an explosive crash. One by one, drawers fell open, emptying their metal contents onto the concrete floor with a deafening cacophony that brought back memories of that fateful night in the desert.

Pain racked his body. Leaning against a nearby post, he willed the fury to subside.

He stared at his bloodied knuckles through a blur of tears, knowing the damage to his heart was far worse.

How dare she compare him to that lowlife she was once married to. Then again, it wasn't as if he was unfamiliar with the distrust caused by past hurts. Otherwise, he wouldn't have accused her of believing him half a man.

Helplessness washed over him like the rain outside the window. It was a feeling he knew well and had vowed he'd never feel again. Right now, though, it was all he had.

Why had Grace let Mama talk her into staying until tomorrow? It was only a little rain.

Lightning flashed and thunder boomed just then, rattling the windows on Roger's garage.

Okay, maybe Mama had a point.

Grace unhooked the bungee cord that secured her footlocker to the tongue of her trailer. She set the trunk on the concrete floor and lifted the lid so she could add a few last-minute items.

It wasn't as if she wanted to leave Mama so soon. Matter of fact, given her heart problems, Grace would just as soon stay. But what choice did she have? Even if she wasn't working for Kaleb anymore, Ouray was tiny. She was bound to run into him. Not to mention that just about every place in town would remind her of him.

Thoughts of the pained expression on his face when

she turned in her resignation this morning had her dinner feeling more like a lead weight in her belly. There was no doubt in her mind that he did indeed love her. But that was now. What about later? What if he changed his mind? She couldn't go through that again.

Thunder cracked overhead.

Grace shot to her feet, wrapping her arms around her stomach. Why had she allowed herself to fall in love? This gut-wrenching ache was exactly why she'd promised herself she'd never open her heart again. Yet she did it anyway. Allowing Kaleb to sneak past her defenses.

The side door opened then and Roger stepped inside. Pushing back the hood of his jacket, he shut the door behind him. "'Tain't a fit night out there for man or beast."

She grinned, thinking about her father. He used to say the same thing. "Sounds like it's getting worse."

"I believe you're right." Shoving his hands into the pockets of his faded jeans, he stepped into the one-car space that had housed her motorcycle and trailer while she stayed with them. "Thought I should check on you. Make sure everything was okay."

"I'm fine." She glanced down at the open footlocker. "Just making sure I'm all set for tomorrow." The cruise line had agreed to look at the possibility of assigning her to another ship. Something that sailed sooner. Even though she might have to take a different job. In the meantime, she'd decided to stay with Lucy in Flagstaff.

He nodded. "I'm sorry you have to leave so soon. I've enjoyed getting to know you."

"Likewise." Embarrassment had her tucking her hands in her back pockets. "It certainly took me long enough."

"Ah, don't worry about it." He hesitated a moment. As though carefully choosing his words. "You know, my, uh, first wife and I didn't have any kids of our own. But if I'd had a daughter, I'd like to think that we would've been as close as you and your father were."

Tears pricked the backs of her eyes, though she quickly blinked them away. "I know this is none of my business, but why did you and Camille choose not to have children?"

"It wasn't our choice." He moved to the small workbench on the far wall, grabbed two stools that were tucked underneath and set them near the trailer. "Have a seat."

Raindrops pelted the window as they sat.

"We tried for years to have a baby. For the longest time, Camille felt as though she'd failed me as a wife."

Grace could definitely relate to that.

"However, nothing could have been further from the truth."

She studied the silver-haired man before her, waiting for him to continue.

"I married Camille because I loved *her* and wanted to share my life with her." Hands clasped in his lap, he continued. "Kids simply would have been an extension of that love. But it never changed."

"Unconditional." Something she'd always heard of, but had never experienced outside of familial relationships. The longer they were married, the more she realized that Aaron's love always seemed to hinge on something. How she dressed or who her friends were or how many toys she'd let him buy. *You want me to be happy, don't you, Grace?*

"That's right. Real love is steadfast. Just like all these mountains." He gestured toward the window that spanned the wide garage door.

"And Cascade Falls." Their steadfastness was what made them so special to Kaleb.

"Exactly."

Roger's wife had been a lucky woman. "Was Camille ever able to accept that you loved her regardless?"

"Over time. God showed her that He had other plans for her life. Like teaching young girls. Mentoring them. By the time she passed away, she had more kids than she'd ever dreamed of."

Grace couldn't help smiling. "I wish I could have known her."

Roger cleared his throat, his expression serious. "Grace, don't let what Aaron did define you. Or any man God might place in your path. We're not all jerks."

She puffed out a laugh.

"God has a plan for you, Grace. Just follow His lead." If she had a nickel for every time she'd heard that…

"That would be easier to do if fear didn't have me in a choke hold."

"I hear ya. However, I know for a fact that God is bigger than our fears. He's chased away more of mine than I care to count."

Another streak of lightning, followed by a loud bang. The lights flickered.

Roger stood. "I think we'd best be getting inside."

She watched the trees dancing wildly on the other side of the window. "I think you're right." She rose and handed him her stool, thinking how much her father would have liked Roger. "Thank you, for being patient with me and for telling me Camille's story."

"You're welcome." The sincerity in his blue eyes made her wonder what had been wrong with her all those years, why she'd refused to accept him.

"And just for the record, I'm really glad Mama married you." Fighting back tears, she wrapped her arms around his waist and hugged him. And he hugged her back.

Later that night, after the rain had passed, Grace lay in

her bed, tucked beneath her grandmother's quilt, thoughts of Kaleb drifting through her mind. Conflicted thoughts. If only he were here. He'd be able to help her sort through them.

Even though that wasn't possible, she still longed for the strength of his embrace and the protection it offered. He was a good man. A godly man. A man who could be trusted. Like Roger.

She replayed his and Camille's story in her mind. What a lucky woman Camille had been to have such a wonderful husband. And Grace couldn't help wondering—

Dear God, is there someone out there who could love me unconditionally?

She closed her eyes, sending tears trailing into her ears. *Someone like Kaleb.*

I do love him, God, and I hate that I've hurt him. But I'm so afraid.

God is bigger than our fears. Roger's words echoed in her mind.

I'm such a mess. God, I've been an idiot to think I could handle life without You. Forgive me. Help me, God. Save me from myself. Right now, I choose to trust You. Remove the fears that have blinded me and show me what it is You would have me do with my life. Whether in Ouray or somewhere else, I want to live the life You would have me live, be the woman You want me to be. Please, God. In Jesus's name.

Opening her eyes, she stared into the blackness. Yet inside, the part of her that had been hollowed out by grief and despair was filled with an incredible light that brightened the darkest corners of her being. She felt alive and whole, for the first time in years.

And it felt amazing.

Chapter Seventeen

Kaleb couldn't sleep. Restless, he'd finally got up and paced his living room for so long he was surprised he hadn't worn a trail in the hardwood. He didn't care, though. He was too busy kicking himself for being so stupid. Instead of telling Grace he wanted her to stay in Ouray, he should have proposed. Reassured her that he loved her, whether they were able to have children or not.

He had to go after her. That was all there was to it. And once he found her, he'd do everything in his power to keep her from leaving again.

Problem was, he had no idea where she'd gone.

Roughing a hand over the stubble that lined his jaw, he glanced at the clock on the wall. Five thirty. Would Roger be up by now, or should he wait until six?

Ah, who cared. He'd waited long enough. Maybe some fresh air would help him piece together his thoughts so he wouldn't sound like a bumbling fool.

Outside, the morning air was still, the streets empty as he hoofed his way to Roger and Donna's. Kaleb couldn't remember ever feeling so torn up inside. Not after his accident, not even when Gina left.

But Grace wasn't Gina. She was the rose to his thorns. The face he looked forward to seeing every morning at work. The one who was his voice of reason, able to talk him down off the ledge. He couldn't imagine life without her.

But what if he couldn't find her? No, she'd tell her mother where she was.

He raked a frustrated hand through his hair. Grace had mentioned something about a change of plans with the cruise line. He thought it was just an excuse. But what if they wanted her to come early? Was she headed there now? If so, where was there?

Groaning, he stopped. Hands on his hips, he looked to the sky. Though still dark for the most part, to the east light was trying to make itself known.

Lord, I need Your help here. Show me what I'm supposed to do.

When he finally made it to Roger's, he noticed there were lights on inside. Good. They were up.

Grabbing hold of the handrail, he made his way onto the wooden porch. Suddenly he found himself hesitating. He'd better knock quietly in case Donna was still asleep.

He rapped on the door, noting the scabs on his knuckles. It had taken him hours yesterday to sort through his tools and put them back into their rightful places inside the tool chest. Served him right for reacting the way he did. Though it had seemed like a good idea at the time.

"Come on." He raised his fist to knock again when the door opened.

"Kaleb?" Roger pushed open the screen door. "What are you doing here? And so early?"

He let go a sigh. "I could really use a friend."

Concern morphed into a smile as Roger stepped out of the way and said, "How about a cup of coffee?"

"How about an entire pot?" Kaleb shoved the door closed behind him, then followed his friend into the mostly white kitchen.

While Roger poured the coffee, Kaleb slumped into one of the four wooden chairs around the kitchen table. "Donna still asleep?"

"Yeah. Since coming home from the hospital, she's taken to sleeping a bit longer." The man handed him a large, steaming mug.

Kaleb inhaled the aroma and took a sip.

Roger settled in the chair across from him. "You look terrible, by the way."

He hadn't looked in the mirror, but— "No doubt."

"So what's going on?"

Kaleb rested his forearms on the table. "I didn't tell you, but Grace quit yesterday. Though, seeing as how she's left town, I'm sure you know that by now."

Roger leaned back in his chair. "Any idea why?"

"She said something about the cruise line having a change of plans, but that may have been just fluff. Because, ultimately, she admitted it was because she couldn't have kids and that I deserved them."

"I see." Roger eyed him over the rim of his cup.

"I told her it didn't matter, that we could adopt."

"And?"

Kaleb's heart twisted. "She said her ex told her the same thing."

Roger leaned forward now. "I understand what you're feeling, Kaleb. I mean, while there wasn't a third party involved, Camille often expressed her regret that she couldn't give me a child." He clasped his hands. "Society tells them that's what they're supposed to do. So when they aren't able to live up to those expectations, they feel as though they've let us down."

"Yeah, well, Grace's ex didn't do me any favors." He took another drink. "Why can't they just believe that they're enough? I didn't say, 'I love you *if* we have kids.' I told her I loved her."

"Do you?"

"Are you kidding? Everything within me is crying out for her. I gotta find her, Roger. Please tell me you know where she's gone."

Something sparked in his friend's gaze and he slowly grinned. "I don't think you'll have to go far."

"What?"

Roger nodded toward the door.

Kaleb whirled around to see Grace standing behind him. He was in such a hurry to stand, he almost toppled his chair. "Grace." He simply stared at her, his breathing ragged.

Grabbing his coffee cup, Roger pushed to his sock feet. "I think I'll leave you two alone."

Still staring, Kaleb wasn't sure whether to hug Grace, kiss her or simply ask her to sit down. Finally, he held out his hand.

Hope flooded through him when she took hold.

He pulled out the chair beside him and she sat down. Without ever letting go of her, he sat, too. "How long were you standing there?"

She smiled then. "Long enough."

He raked his free hand through his hair. A move he'd done so often, it was probably standing on end like Roger's. But he didn't care. Grace was all that mattered. "How come you're still here?"

"Mama wanted me to wait until the rain passed." She shrugged. "And I needed a little more time with her."

He wasn't sure he wanted to know the answer to his next question, but he'd ask it anyway. "Are you still planning to leave?"

Her beautiful hazel eyes bored into him. "I don't know. Is there a reason for me to stay?"

He brushed his thumb over her knuckles. "I didn't know what my life was missing until you walked into it. And now I don't want to live without you." Scooting to the edge of his seat, he eased down onto his good knee. "I guess what I'm trying to say is, I want to marry you, Grace. And spend forever with you." Looking up at her, he took hold of her other hand, clasping them between both of his. "Grace McAllen, will you marry me?"

Tears welled in her eyes. "Yes." Pulling her hands free, she cupped his cheeks. "You have shown me the true meaning of love, Kaleb Palmer. You taught me to trust again. In God, in love. In you. I love you and I would be proud to be your wife."

Standing, he took her into his arms and kissed her. Best of all, she kissed him back. Without fear or reservation.

When they finally parted, he couldn't stop smiling. Until he remembered— "What about the cruise line? Your contract?"

She laid a hand against his chest. "As I said yesterday, there's been a change in plans."

"I thought you were just saying that."

She shook her head. "No. I got an email Sunday. They said that, due to unforeseeable circumstances, they were going to have to push our sail date into November. Making my contract null and void, unless I signed an amendment."

"Did you?"

"Not yet."

He nearly choked. "You mean you're still considering it?"

"Not really. Because now I'm thinking that November might be a good time for a wedding."

"Sweetheart, if you're talking about you and me, I'm ready whenever you are."

Epilogue

Grace could hardly believe her ears. Sure, she hadn't felt good since shortly after she and Kaleb returned from their honeymoon in Cancún in November, but she figured it was because she drank the water. Throw in the hubbub of the holidays and anyone would feel a little off-kilter. But this…

"Say that again, Doctor."

He looked at her with a quirky grin. "Mrs. Palmer, not only are you pregnant, the sonogram showed two heartbeats. You're having twins."

"Trent, you need to do me a favor and keep this to yourself, while I figure out a creative way to deliver this news to my husband."

Dr. Lockridge, husband of Kaleb's friend Blakely, laughed. "No worries, Grace. However, I expect to see him with you during your next visit."

Grace practically fell into her new SUV, disbelief still swirling around her. She laid a hand against her belly. She was actually pregnant. With twins!

Kaleb was going to be beside himself. But this wasn't the kind of news she could blurt out in a single statement. This was the kind of thing that needed to be savored a little bit at a time.

And if it involved a little fun on her part, at her husband's expense, so be it.

Okay, first she'd need to make a couple of stops on the way home. Then project baby bomb was under way.

First stop, the market, where she picked up a few items. Then it was on to the hardware store.

Kaleb was so perceptive, though. She was going to be hard-pressed to keep this from him. Not that she planned on waiting forever. After all, a girl could only keep a secret from her husband for so long.

She pulled into the drive, excitement and anticipation vying for center stage. Drawing in a deep breath, she grabbed her bags and headed inside.

"Hey, sweetheart." Kaleb met her at the door and gave her a quick kiss. "What did the doctor have to say?"

"Um, he said I've been drinking too much water."

"Too much water? I didn't think that was possible."

"Apparently it is." She turned to hide her smile. "So what are you working on?"

"Same thing I was when you left. Stripping the wallpaper in the dining room." He slinked out of the kitchen, still not thrilled about giving up his home gym. Fortunately, a gift certificate from his parents to the gym at the hot springs seemed to help soften the blow.

She grabbed her bag from the market, pulled out two pears and gave them a quick rinse. "Hey."

He turned back around.

"How 'bout a snack." She tossed one his way before taking a bite of her own.

He glanced at it. "What's this?"

"A pear, silly. We should start thinking in pairs."

Confusion marred his handsome features. "Are you sure you're okay?"

"Couldn't be better."

A while later, she called him back into the bedroom that still contained all those boxes of memorabilia. "What do you think about one of these colors for this room?" She fanned out several pastel paint chips.

"Grace, I thought we were going to hold off on this room until we finished the others?"

She shrugged. "I know. I just wondered what colors you might like."

To his credit, he studied them. "They don't really go with what we have planned for the rest of the house."

"I know, but I thought we could have a little fun with this space."

He rubbed the back of his neck. "If you say so."

Grace wanted so badly to spill the beans, but forced herself to wait a little longer.

In the spirit of celebration, she prepared seared steak for dinner.

"Kaleb, honey, would you check the oven for me, please?" She really did appreciate the fact that he insisted on helping with meals.

"What's this?"

He held up a hamburger bun.

She had to bite her tongue to keep from laughing. "Looks like somebody put a bun in our oven."

"A bun with steak? That's the most—"

She could almost see the lightbulb flicker to life.

His mouth fell open. "Grace? Did you? Do we?"

Unable to contain her secret anymore, she nodded, her grin from ear to ear. "You are going to be a daddy, my love." She threw her arms around his neck as he lifted her off the floor.

"So that's what these weird things you've been saying were all about."

"Uh-huh."

He spun her around the kitchen. "We're going to have a baby. We're going to have a baby!"

She couldn't resist just one more opportunity to mess with him. "Sort of."

He set her on the floor. "What do you mean, sort of? We're not going to have, like, puppies or something, are we?"

"Not that I'm aware of. However, I was wondering— how many car seats do you think we can fit in the back of the Jeep?"

The countless reactions that crossed his face were absolutely priceless. "Grace?" That deep voice meant it was time for her to come clean.

"According to the doctor, I am pregnant. With twins."

Those same reactions she'd seen just a moment ago returned with a vengeance. His hand fell to her belly. "Twins?"

"Yep." She slipped out of his embrace and snagged her purse from the counter. Then she pulled out the picture of the sonogram and handed it to Kaleb. "Baby A and baby B." She pointed.

He ran a hand through his hair as he exited the kitchen, still staring at the picture, and headed toward the living room. "Two babies?" He dropped onto their new, slipcovered sofa. "This is amazing."

Grace curled up beside him. "Trust me, I was every bit as stunned as you are."

He wrapped an arm around her and pulled her to him. "So when are you—"

"August. Which means we'll need to make plans for the shop. Perhaps we could get Mama and Roger to fill in for a while."

"I have a feeling that won't be a problem." He pulled

her into his lap. "I love you, Grace. And just when I think I can't love you any more, you blow me out of the water."

Her hand caressed his cheek. "I guess God had something bigger in store for us."

"Even if he hadn't, I'd still love you with everything I have. These babies are just an extension of that love."

Tears sprang to her eyes as she remembered what Roger had told her about Camille that night in his garage. Camille was a blessed woman. And so was Grace.

God had a plan for her. All she had to do was entrust Him with that plan. And even if children hadn't been a part of it, He had brought her into a new life. One filled with happiness and love and the hope of brighter tomorrows.

* * * * *

Dear Reader,

Some books are easier to write than others. Kaleb and Grace's story was not one of them. During the course of their story, I faced many struggles, both as a writer and as a person. God is good, though, and I am so pleased with the way this story ultimately turned out.

God did not promise us a life free of problems. However, He has promised to walk with us, even carry us, through the strife that is so prevalent in this world. And whether our wounds are physical, as Kaleb's were, or the unseen scars that Grace bore, God is able to bring healing in ways we might never have imagined if we simply put our trust in Him.

I hope you enjoyed *Falling for the Hometown Hero* and, if you've read any of my other stories, returning to Ouray. It's still one of my most favorite places on earth and one that will forever hold a very special place in my heart. Let's journey there together again very soon.

Until then, I would love to hear from you. You can contact me via my website, www.mindyobenhaus.com, or you can snail-mail me c/o Love Inspired Books, 195 Broadway, 24th Floor, New York, NY 10007.

See you next time,
Mindy

REQUEST YOUR FREE BOOKS!

2 FREE INSPIRATIONAL NOVELS
PLUS 2
FREE
MYSTERY GIFTS

Love Inspired®

"So you didn't like it here?" Vic asked. "Coming every summer?"

"I missed my friends back home, but there were parts I liked."

"I remember seeing you girls in church on Sunday."

"Part of the deal," Lauren said, a faint smile teasing her mouth. "And I didn't mind that part, either. The message was always good, once I started really listening. I can't remember who the pastor was, but what he said resonated with me."

"Jodie and Erin would attend some of the youth events, didn't they?"

"Erin more than any of us."

"I remember my brother Dean talking about her," Vic said. "I think he had a secret crush on her."

"He was impetuous, wasn't he?"

"That's being kind. But he's settled now."

Thoughts of Dean brought up the same problem that had brought him to the ranch.

His deal with Lauren's father.

"So, I hate to be a broken record," he continued, "but

I was wondering if I could come by the house tomorrow. To go through your father's papers."

Lauren sighed.

Vic tamped down his immediate apology. He had nothing to feel bad about. He was just looking out for his brother's interests.

"Yes. Of course. Though—" She stopped herself there. "Sorry. You probably know better what you're looking for."

Vic shot her a glance across the cab of the truck. "I'm not trying to jeopardize your deal. When I first leased the ranch from your father, it was so that my brother could have his own place. And I'm hoping to protect that promise I made him. Especially now. After his accident."

"I understand," Lauren said, her smile apologetic. "I know what it's like to protect siblings."

"Are you the oldest?"

"Erin and I are twins, but I'm older by twenty minutes."

Lauren smiled at him. And as their eyes held, he felt it again. An unexpected rush of attraction. When her eyes grew ever so slightly wider, he wondered if she felt it, too.

He dragged his attention back to the road.

You're no judge of your feelings, he reminded himself, his hands tightening on the steering wheel as if reining in his attraction to this enigmatic woman.

He'd made mistakes in the past, falling for the wrong person. He couldn't do it again. He couldn't afford to.

Especially not with Lauren.